THE NOTES BETWEEN US

SHIRLEY DAY

First published in 2026 by Bloodhound Books.

www.bloodhoundbooks.com

Print ISBN: 978-1917705639

CHAPTER 1

CLARA

The golden doors of the lift glide open, and out spills yet another wave of gorgeous women clad in designer heels and clingy dresses. People might find it odd, but I could seriously watch this kind of show all day. It's times like this that I love my job on reception. This place can be so swanky. It's like being at some high-end fashion event, and from the hungry look on Stan the doorman's face, I figure he feels the same way. Only most likely for different reasons. Is that a twitch of his lips? He surely can't be about to whistle.

'Stan,' I hiss.

He winks. As usual, he was pulling my leg. The man is sixty if he's a day, and a full-on joker. I have to watch myself constantly because Stan's main remit, after opening doors and tipping that peaked cap of his, appears to be to make me laugh. I sometimes think working the door all day has turned Stan's poor old brain into jelly. It's the boredom. Because when there are no auditions, that revolving door can be kind of quiet. If I stay here too long, I could end up just like him – squeezing the everyday for just a squidge of funny.

I've been here almost a year now. It was okay at first. Initially, there was a lot to do, and I like being busy. The steel and glass building of Delagado Towers may have only been up for ten years, and the fittings might still be fancy, but when I arrived here, the systems were antiquated. As soon as I got my feet under the desk, I gave the entire reception area a total revamp. First, I tackled the call centre, working through the operator panels and switchboards in the rented offices. With a bit of help from tech support, I gradually figured out how everything connected. So, if clients called up, I could see who they were on my screen, and if I knew which firm they represented, I could normally figure out who they wanted before I even picked up the phone. I'd then answer with the name of the relevant company and direct them with absolutely no fuss to the right person. I can't help it; organisation is my thing. I love it when a system works effortlessly, any kind of system. I was brought up by my older brother, Minty, who I absolutely love to bits, but when sensible was being handed out, that boy must have missed the memo. Chaos when describing my brother is an understatement. His mind is permanently tied up with something else, so ever since I could push a Hoover, wipe a pot, or puff a sofa pillow, organisation on the home front landed at my door. That's why, when I first got the job here, it was a perfect fit. There was plenty to overhaul. After I'd tackled the call centre, I sank my teeth into the booking procedure for the conference rooms. I even introduced a new online system so anyone wanting to reserve a room could find availability in just a few clicks. Modern tech, I just love it. And don't even get me started on the front desk. When I first arrived, there were drawers stuffed with a host of curiously useless things, but I cleared them all out – every last forgotten paperclip. These days, everything is running smooth and sleek, just the way I like it.

Only now that it all works like a dream, guess what? I'm as bored as it's possible to be without finding yourself six feet under, and Stan, since he stands there watching me for most of the day, knows. He gives the wide, glass revolving door to the outside a jaunty push with his white-gloved hand in anticipation of the next batch of ladies. Of course, he's spun it too hard. If the bevvy of beauties heading to or from the top floor were to put one kitten-heeled shoe into that swing-door matrix, they'd get caught in a whirlwind of centrifugal force. Luckily, the last batch deposited from the lifts are strolling across the wide marble atrium in front of me. It'll be a while before they get to Stan and his white-gloved antics. He's just trying to get their attention; he'll be tap dancing for them next.

'Lanyards,' I call, as they move past in a cloud of scent.

The beauties giggle, unwinding the straps of their day passes from their long, elegant necks.

'Oh my gosh,' a tall girl with hazel eyes as wide as a forest says. 'You are so lucky working here.'

I smile as if to say, *yes, aren't I?* But I know that I'm just a nothing and a nobody, just a face people walk past.

'How did it go?' I ask, eager for news of the seventeenth floor, the music emporium of Delagado Design.

'Oh, fantastic.' A beanpole of a woman clutches her hands across her tanned, stretched chest. 'Fingers crossed.'

'Thank you *soooo* much,' one hazel-eyed stunner intones.

'Yes, so much,' the other women chorus.

And peeling off their lanyards, every one of them nods appreciatively at me as they click-clack past, forgetting my existence once I'm out of sight.

I guess I'm kind of the gatekeeper here at Delagado Towers, which is pretty impressive if you're from Middle Earth. Gatekeepers have big business in the Tolkien storyline, but it's not so impressive if you happen to be living in Wapping. Gatekeeper, receptionist. I may have sorted out the admin system for the building, but on the seventeenth floor, they remain oblivious to my existence. The women floating past my desk, on the other hand, love me fleetingly because they are gloriously unaware (and uninterested) as to the fact that I have nothing to do with Delagado Design – the high-end music production suite that straddles the entire top floor of the building – the place where they've all just been auditioning, singing their hearts out.

I grab my clipboard, ready to mark off more incoming lanyards. That's all part of my job: I check them in and check them out. I have a mountain of work to do before I can knock off tonight. It's our busy time. With my hands wrapped in the stiff black cords of the photo IDs, I gaze wistfully after the women. Some girls get all the luck. I glance down at the list of women auditioning who haven't checked back out. I have a heap missing in action. There must be a party load still up there on the seventeenth floor. I sigh, sinking down onto my hard but sleek bar stool seat, pillowing my chin on my hands as I stare towards the bank of golden lifts. If only I had the guts to join them, wander over to the elevator doors, those portals to stardom, and zoom into the stratosphere. Because I can sing. I love to sing. It's the one thing that I seriously enjoy. Only…

'Oi, you.' Stan beams at me. 'Quit your daydreaming. There'll be another gaggle along soon.'

Heat floods my cheeks. Trust Stan to catch me when my brain's addled and on a time-out vacation. A person could spend their life dreaming away the hours on reception. But that's not going to do anyone any good. I straighten, grabbing a stack of visitor passes with a sniff.

'Receptionist by day,' he says jovially, 'songbird by night.'

I shouldn't have told Stan about my secret passion. He loves to tease, but I've never said I had designs on being a diva. That's not for me. Not with my stage fright.

'I do love singing, Stan,' I say firmly, 'but only in the choir.'

'Choir.' He shrugs. 'How different can it be? You're using the same instrument. Those, what are they called? Vocal cord things. Why not take the lift up? Throw your hat into the ring. Confidence, Clara, my sweet, that's all you need.' He chuckles, his brown eyes crinkling at the corners. 'You could catch on the tail end of this little lot here,' he whispers as a further bevy of beauties pours through his door.

I shoot him a wry look. 'Couldn't go leaving my desk. I'm an integral part of the process.'

'Come on, Clara,' he says, grinning. 'Why not show us what you've got? Use that golden voice of yours and direct this next batch to the right floor before we get a queue down the street.'

I craftily stick my tongue out at him before plastering on a smile to greet another flock of starlets. Of course, he's right to bring me back to earth. By suggesting I hop in a lift and take a bid for stardom, he's challenging me, and it's a challenge I'm not about to take. There's no point in crying over missed opportunities. I need to get on with the job in hand. In truth, it's about time I woke up to the fact that my voice is only fit for being helpful. I am the nice woman at the end of the telephone line, the meet and greet over the reception desk – I couldn't do what they do. Yes, I sing in a choir, but singing solo, standing up on some stage with just a mic, I'd never have the nerve. Besides, I look nothing like these women. We are poles apart. They could, in fact, be a different species. These women are magazine perfect, with their flawless skin, hair and teeth, and I'm... Hmm, I tilt my head to one side and stare at my reflection in one of the long windows. As always, I feel disappointed by what I see – a short, everyday-looking young woman handing out passes to a bevy of glorious beauties. I guess my hair's pretty: blonde, long, wavy. But then again, my body's kind of wavy too, and I'm not convinced bodies are supposed to be wavy. Certainly not the way mine is. Compared to the women auditioning, I know I'm not worth pausing to look at.

I give myself a shake. That kind of mindset is not helpful.

'I think I'm going to tidy out the cupboards,' I say to Stan.

'To your heart's content,' Stan calls after me as I scoot my way along to the end of my desk and open the cupboard I use for stationery. I should make a new order. I grab a manuscript pad, but as I do, an item I gained courtesy of my older (less sensible) brother falls to the floor – a Halloween mask. It was on my first day working here that my brother Minty showed up at the Towers wearing the mask. He is an impossible joker with a seriously unfunny repertoire. So much worse than Stan's. My brother is always plotting up some funny scheme and itching to play me. Practical jokes are part of the guy's DNA. So, it's something I know I have to grin and bear because underneath all the whoopie cushions, electric handshakes, and cling film over the toilet bowl, my brother has a heart of gold. Okay, so he's a wee bit messy to live with and has a problem throwing anything out, but he's been everything to me all through my life. With my parents gone, it can't have been easy in his situation, staying at home to babysit your sister when all your mates are going out. The practical jokes were a small price to pay. Besides, Minty was easy to spot when he had a joke brewing. Normally, you caught his laughter before you saw what he was up to. I'd managed to confiscate the mask as soon as I saw him coming through the glass doors. I should have hurled it by now, but just like my brother, I do hate to throw things away. Only, unlike Minty, I believe in re-housing. Someone will be glad of it. The thing needs to grab a lift to a charity shop. If it finds its way home, Minty's bound to do something daft with it again.

'Discover anything interesting?' Stan calls from beside the door.

It's then that it hits me, a smile spreading over my face. A smile so wide and so big that even my brother would be proud of me. Stan may be a practical joker, but I have life-long experience from my brother. Maybe what Stan needs is a dash of his own medicine. Pulling on the mask, I jump from behind the counter, throw back my head, and let out a growl.

Suddenly, I hear the lift doors slide open.

'Hey, you,' comes a deep male voice.

I freeze. My heart skipping a beat. It's Marco Delagado, the ultra-smooth record producer from the top floor. He's reflected in the smoky windows, swaying slightly, a bottle in his hand. He has his back to me, so all I can really see is the side of his face, but wow is he gorgeous. Dark wavy hair, a chiselled chin with one of those film-star cracked cleft things that are so macho. He's tall, with every bone of his body encased in a great wedge of wrapped muscle. Why had no one told me there was a God working at the top of the building?

'Get some food sent up,' he orders gruffly towards Stan.

Stan's eyes are looking panic-stricken, going from Marco to me, me to Marco. And as the man turns slowly around, I realise I'm still wearing the stupid mask.

'My God,' Marco says with an air of disdain. 'A goblin! The receptionists these days are as ugly as sin.'

He stumbles back into the elevator, leaving me cowering behind my mask.

'Phew,' Stan says. 'Thank goodness you had that mask on, hey? If you'd shown him your naked face, we would have been in serious trouble. Think you just got trolled.'

MARCO

It's getting late. Five o'clock, and we've had no one. Not one voice in a gruelling two-week period has made my pulse race. Because that's what it's all about – emotional connection for the masses, and I'm the guy who has to feel it first. To spot the potential. If I'm going to tell the press, the media, that I've found the next big thing, *the* female vocalist of the year, I have to have something in my pocket and that 'something' has to be big, beautiful, and easy to sell. The kind of 'something' that makes people sit up and take notice. Different. Knock your socks off great. But no. That hasn't been happening. Sure, if push comes to shove we can mix the voice up. Post-production can make anyone sound two hundred per cent better than a sad warble fresh from the lips. Even if a girl hasn't got a great look, we can fix that, but by five o'clock on week two, I'm losing my will to live. We've been at it since eight in the morning. I don't do mornings. Then, to top it all, this girl comes into the recording studio and I cannot believe what I'm seeing. I mean, she looks like a horse, and that's not an insult. I can do insults. So, no, this would be a statement of fact. She's got this horse's head mask thing pulled down over her face. I mean, it's a gimmick, obviously. She wants me to remember her, and I will, only for all the wrong reasons.

'Okay,' I tell her, trying to smile. They've got me on camera too. The whole thing will get edited down and televised. Yours truly streamed into the living rooms of the nation with a host of warbling beauties. 'The horse is cute.' I manage a thin smile. The 'cute' thing is a lie. The horse is stupid. I mean, feathers? Maybe. A funky hat? Yes. Cat's ears? That can work, but a horse's head. At best, it says 'Mafia, the godfather', and at worst, it comes across as seriously deluded. But I need to keep calm and say it looks good because if they use this footage, they'll put the content out before the watershed, and kids love horses. That's probably why she's wearing the headdress. She wants to make it through to the final cut. My motivation for keeping calm is slightly different. I want to make it through without looking like an arsehole. I'm not an arsehole, despite rumours to the contrary. It's not personal; it goes with the territory. Everyone hates you if you're born with a silver spoon in your mouth. It's wrong. It's a deeply misguided form of prejudice, but hey, will anyone believe me on that? Of course not. There's no sympathy for the rich kid. So, I tell the girl with the stupid horse hat/mask/face that it's cute. Selling my soul yet again.

'What have you got for us then?' I glance down the list of

names on my call sheet. 'Tianna.' God, where do they get these names from?

Tianna smiles. She's got big teeth. I wonder if I should compliment her on those as well?

'Milly Stylish,' she says. 'Everlasting Eyes.'

Yeah, of course it is, I think, leaning back in my chair. Milly Stylish has been in the top ten for the past six months. I've heard four different versions of this exact same song today. Has no one got anything new? The horsewoman will soon be breathing all over the microphone, whispering the lyrics out like she's got a fur ball in her throat. Just like good old Milly. Don't get me wrong, Milly Stylish is brilliant. She's the original. Truly stylish. Got her own thing going on. But this?

Tianna starts singing. I phase out until the horsewoman bleats three flat notes in a row. There's barely any song left to murder. There's surely an easier way to make a living. 'Know what?' I say, getting to my feet. 'I think maybe, maybe we need a break.'

I know they're all looking at me like I'm an entitled idiot. I don't care. I need a reality check. A shot of normal. 'Think we all need a little something to eat,' I say, stretching my gym-toned arms behind my neck. They are gym-toned; that's not just me hyping my body up for no good reason. I have the best personal trainer in town. I hate personal training. Seriously loathe it, only guess what? I wish I were doing press-ups now rather than listening to… whatever it is coming out of horse girl's mouth. 'Stay there. Give me five.' I walk out of the booth and head for the lifts. Not my lift – the lift that takes me from my parking spot to the seventeenth floor. No. Reality is different. Reality comes in through the main doors, and sometimes it's good to remind myself of that fact.

I get into the golden elevator and press zero. The lift jerks into action and has me sliding down towards planet Earth. I grin at my face reflected in the cube of mirrors. Okay, so I've been drinking. In fact, I appear to have a bottle attached to one arm.

The alcohol is certainly making me snappy. It was a bad idea to hit the booze, but in my defence, I'm pretty sure it would have been impossible to get through one more day of auditions without drowning my senses in a few shots of highly expensive single malts. Okay, so maybe it's been more than a few shots, but who's counting?

The zero light above the door pings into action, indicating I've hit ground level as the lift glides to a halt. Slowly, the doors slide back. I'm always impressed by the foyer; it has more marble than an Italian mountain. My dad was responsible for the design. I can't take the credit. In truth, I can't take credit for much around here. My existence is an inherited hand-me-down: lucrative, flash, but with very little wiggle room for forging a personality. I've spent my life under the eye of the press. Being wealthy appears to have made me public property. Maybe that's why I normally sneak up and down in my own elevator. I don't want to be seen, I don't want to be on show, and I don't want to be reminded of my rich old sod of a father. He might have been well and truly loaded, but he was not a nice man, saving his truly worst bits for his nearest and dearest.

As we hit the ground floor and the lift door opens, I catch sight of the guy standing in the revolving doorway in that same spot – the old one, with the wrinkled smile and cheeky grin. He's been working here for years. I should know his name, but since I never use that door, there's no point.

'Hey, you,' I shout at him before I've even left the comfort of my mirrored cage. 'Get some food sent up.' I'm not sure if this is his job or not, and to be perfectly honest, I don't care. If I tell someone to do something anywhere in this building, it will get done – my name's over the door.

The guy's looking odd. Doing some kind of ping-pong thing with his eyes. Shifting them rapidly from left to right.

I follow his gaze, and seriously, I could scream. There's this… Actually, I'm not even one hundred per cent sure what it is. Neck down, it's nice. Some woman, curvy as hell. I like my women curvy. Fashion, music, and the world I work in, those curvy types of women are few and far between. She's dressed all in blue, the kind of soft woollen material that makes you want to stroke it. It's one of those wrap-dress things. The ones that accentuate any attributes. Not that she needs to do any *accentuating* – there's a lot going on without requiring any added extras. But her face, her head? I mean – I have a horse woman up in the studio and now this! It feels like today I have truly seen it all, but I have no idea what the hell this receptionist's got covering her face. What is this, some kind of fashion trend? It's not even Halloween, and this isn't even an arty space. Creative dressing is okay in creative spaces, but this is the foyer of the swankiest building in town, housing some of the most important industries. Some women will stop at nothing to get themselves noticed.

'My God,' I stutter, horrified. She's got this beautiful body, and then she sticks some kind of atrocity on top of it. What the hell is happening in the fashion industry? Maybe I should be paying more attention. 'Why…?' And for a moment, I stall because that's enough. All I want to say is 'why?' The world seems to have gone mad. Luckily, I've had a fair few drinks and, like most men in my circle, I'm never short of a quick quip when my head's buzzing, so I let rip, announcing, 'Receptionists these days are as ugly as sin.'

I stumble back into the elevator, leaving what I think must have been the life-size goblin with the great body whimpering behind me and hoping that the guy in the revolving doors got the food order I'd managed to bark out. Reassuring myself, as the elevator pulls me back to my floor, that a) I'll never risk dropping down seventeen levels again, and b) nothing that happens street level is relevant anymore. I thought it was crazy in the studio, but ground level is a whole heap worse.

CHAPTER 2

CLARA

When six thirty comes, I'm reaching for my coat and the hideous Halloween mask. Forget the charity shop; that thing is going straight in the bin.

'Don't take it personally,' Stan says as I walk towards the door, mask in hand. He points one finger up towards the ceiling as though to indicate the seventeenth floor. 'That guy's not exactly an oil painting himself.'

This is clearly not true. Marco Delagado is gorgeous. The sort of gorgeous that album covers are made of.

'Yeah.' I laugh, joining in with the lie. But I have to admit it sounds half-hearted. The man may not be stepping out of an 18th century masterpiece, but he's photoshoot-ready. What's wrong with me, putting that stupid mask on in the first place? All because I wanted to play a joke on Stan. It wasn't even a good joke. I could kick myself. Never mind working on reception, I should be down in the cellar.

There's still a straggle of people up at the studios. Musicians are the type to linger. If I stayed at my desk till the last one came down, I'd be there all night. The night porter can check them off. I've had enough for one day. Besides, I'm looking forward to choir practice and putting the goblin greeting disaster behind me.

❧

When I emerge from the Tube station, the crisp evening air fills my lungs. Practical jokes aside, work is okay. Really it is. Although it sometimes feels as though Delagado Towers is not part of the real world. As though the entire glass and granite construction is simply a gilded cage, and I'm not even the bird on the swing. I'm just the hired elf, poking seed in between the bars to help keep the whole thing turning. But that's okay; real life isn't glamorous, at least not for me.

The church is only a ten-minute ride from work. It's an old stone building nestled between shops that closed hours ago and takeaways that are only just starting to spice up the air. We rehearse in the crypt, which sounds kind of creepy but, in reality, it's a wonderful space with high vaulted ceilings that make your spirit soar, and the smell is incredible. Uplifting. Candle wax, incense, and the assorted perfumes of at least thirty salt-of-the-earth women ranging in age from seventeen to ninety-one. We're an eclectic bunch. Not glamorous, like the women I saw going for auditions today, but with genuine smiles and warm personalities. I've been doing it for years and know we're all here for each other. Song, harmony, and support are what this small group is all about. Who needs wealth, stardom, and golden lifts?

When I pull open the heavy oak door, most of the choir members are already there. Luckily, practice hasn't started yet. Everyone turns towards me in a warm greeting.

'Clara,' someone calls out in welcome. I don't see who it is, simply wave my hand in the general direction it came from and wallow in the heartfelt smiles and nods that the group aim my way. These people are like a second family to me. Evelyn, our choir director, always says that it's the notes between us that keep us strong, and maybe there is something in that. Every time I walk through the door, hear the sound of somebody practicing a scale, I always feel at home. There's a low murmur of chatter, people catching up on the events of the day as women stand in clusters reviewing the sheet music for this week's hymns. Occasionally, someone will open their mouth and trill a few notes.

I stash my coat and bag under a pew as Evelyn waves me over with a smile. I love Evelyn. She may only be three years older than me, but she is so talented, and not just on the music front. Whereas my life still feels embryonic, Evelyn appears to have hers all mapped out. As choir leader, she's doing something she loves. She has a gorgeous baby, a lovely home, and a to-die-for husband. As for me, I have none of these things. The job at Delagado Towers is not a forever career, and I'm still living with my brother – when I say my brother, I also mean his contraptions. The man has a mountain of junk: bits of cars, washing machines, electrical gadgets. His idea of bliss is taking something mechanical apart and then putting it together again. Only the putting-together part doesn't always work.

I stare over at Evelyn, who is smiling reassuringly at a young woman going over some tricky bars. 'You've got it.' She smiles, slipping her hand reassuringly onto the woman's shoulder. 'Just don't get overconfident. That's when you go sharp.'

Overconfidence! I wish I had even a little of that in me.

'Try the A4 once more?' Evelyn suggests, leaning her head to the side. The girl sings. 'You got it,' Evelyn trills.

The girl smiles and nods, pleased with herself. Evelyn is in her element, and this evening, she gets to go home to her perfect family. Some girls get all the luck. Not that I begrudge Evelyn for having her life sorted. I'd just like the same game plan for myself.

'Glad you could make it,' Evelyn says, cheery as always, as she catches my eye. 'We're still missing a soprano, so I'm putting you on first chair tonight.'

First chair! I feel my heart flutter against my ribs in a wave of panic. It's a solo of sorts, even if it is only for a hymn rather than standing in front of a microphone on the seventeenth floor of Delagado Towers, but there's a problem. I don't do solos. I'm not ready. My throat clenches and suddenly I feel short of breath.

'Oh, Evelyn, I can't...' I mumble as my body sinks under my weight, my shoulders caving forward.

My knees go weak, my palms melt, and my breath catches in my throat, and that is only when I'm talking, never mind singing solo! In an instant, I am a dishevelled mess. Along with the physical symptoms of full-on panic attack, there's also a large helping of irritation – I could kick myself for going to pieces. I'm an organised, competent person, but ask me to sing solo and I fall apart. It's just not fair. I just don't like being out in front. I can't even muster up a PowerPoint presentation without dissolving into a blubbering mess. Most days, I'm confident. I can apply myself to almost any situation. Get it sorted. Iron it out. Pull a practical solution out of a minefield of chaos. Didn't I organise reception so that it's never worked better? Aren't I the chief homemaker in the house, making sure my older brother is fed, watered, and dressed in something that's at least part-way clean? But singing – the one thing I truly love – solo terrifies me.

Sensing my panic, Evelyn rests a gentle hand on my arm and whispers, 'You're ready, Clara. Just remember, this is a safe space. We're all here to support each other.'

I glance around at the smiling faces. Twenty-nine of them. Each and every one willing me on, knowing how difficult I find this. I take a deep breath and nod – Evelyn's right. I've been coming to choir practice for two years. I love it. I love the people. If I'm going to do a solo anywhere, here would be the place.

'Okay, everyone,' Evelyn says, raising her voice above the chatter. 'Let's begin with "Amazing Grace". Sopranos, remember to come in strong on that first verse. But before we start, let's just warm up those voices. Are we ready to make some music?'

'Yes!' we chorus back.

Evelyn steps up to the podium, baton in hand.

You can do this, I think to myself as we run effortlessly through some scales. As the notes rise and circle the air, I remember Stan's words – his teasing about my golden voice. Is the sole extent of my talent ushering people to and from the lifts at Delagado Towers? No. No, it's not. I can sing. Practising with the choir has proved that to me. I just need to believe in myself. Sometimes you have to be brave.

With the vocal warm-up done, our pianist, the grey-haired but surprisingly sprightly Ms Migs, strikes up the familiar melody – one that we've sung many times before. Heads held high, eyes all on Evelyn, mouths and throats open wide, the voices around me begin to swell, each section blending in perfect harmony. This is it. My moment. My solo.

I fill my lungs, tilt back my head, part my lips and sing.

CHAPTER 3

CLARA

'That's fantastic,' Minty says, shoving aside some kind of oil-smeared overall from the front passenger seat so I can sit down. It's getting dark and beginning to drizzle as the street lamps flicker on, so the lift home, even in my brother's old rust bucket, is welcome. Besides, there's nothing I love more than seeing Minty's smiling face at the end of the day.

'You did it, doll, your first solo! Knew you could nail it.'

I smile to myself. He has so much belief in me – too much. 'I'm not sure I nailed it...' In truth, I may be talking it down, but I can't help myself – I'm still beaming from the experience.

My brother flips on the indicator, glances over his shoulder, and pulls out into the road. The car groans in response. It's an old Ford. A very old Ford. Minty calls it vintage, but that would be too kind. Fix Or Repair Daily – it's all in the name. But I get the feeling Minty kind of likes the constant struggle to keep it on the road. My brother is a man who enjoys a challenge.

'You sing like an angel, C,' he says enthusiastically. 'Seriously. No exaggeration.'

He always calls me C, as if familiarity has rubbed away all the other letters in my name.

The lights fly past, the familiar streets pulsing outside the rain-streaked windows in a blur of colours. 'You are a little bit biased, Minty, what with being my brother.'

In reality, Minty is so much more than *biased* and so much more than my brother. After our musician parents died tragically on the way back from a gig, it was Minty who made sure we stayed together. He had only just turned nineteen, but Minty brought me up with a dogged determination and a smile. No matter the mishap, he was always there. He made it to every school parents' evening, and parents' evenings had never been his thing, but Minty took the responsibility of raising his scrappy ten-year-old sister seriously. He made sure I was never without, taking on a series of extra jobs, from home removal to Saturday sales assistant. When necessary, Minty even wore a shirt and tie. My brother is not a shirt-and-tie person. All Minty ever really wanted to do was fiddle with engines, but somehow, he managed to fit it all in. He even cooked every evening, ensuring we sat at the table each night for a debrief on my day. He must have read somewhere something about broccoli being necessary for life. So, every mealtime, out came the broccoli. Even today, we have it with pizza.

I glance at him as he steers the car through the familiar streets: his fierce, angular jaw; his tuft of unruly toilet brush hair; his glittering, proud eyes. Even now, when I could easily get a bus home, Minty drops whatever he's doing so he can pick me up from choir practice. So he can be there to hear my news.

'You've got serious talent.' He grins.

'You didn't even hear me.' I laugh.

'Heard you in the shower.' Minty shrugs. 'Just speaking the truth, little sis,' he says nonchalantly.

'How's the house looking?' I ask. I'm hoping he hasn't been busy with another oil-smattered project.

'Yeah. Pretty good.' He nods. 'Just a few bits in the sink.'

I glance over at him and can't help but smile. When I was

seven years old, Minty decided to take apart the washing machine to see 'how it worked'. Only he forgot to put it back together before Mum got home from a shift she occasionally stood in for at the local supermarket. Mum had found Minty sitting in the middle of a pile of tangled wires and bolts, grinning from ear to ear. 'I learnt such a lot!' That was all he said.

After my parents died, money was tight. It was always make-do and mend, but Minty seemed to go that extra mile. He'd tried fixing up an old bike he found at the scrapyard, intending it as a surprise for my birthday. But when he tested it out, the pedals jammed, and poor Minty went careering down the high street, narrowly missing an old woman with her groceries. The bike was beyond repair. After that little mishap, I said I hated bikes in an attempt to avoid mechanical interventions. To this day, I don't even drive.

'So, Clara…'

Hmm, I'm not so keen on that tone of voice. He hardly ever calls me Clara. I know where this is going. 'No.'

Minty takes a moment to peel his eyes from the road and shoot me a look. 'You don't even–'

I feel my eyes narrow. 'I don't need you to fix me up with one of your mates.'

This was beginning to be a bit of a problem. In his desire to fix, Minty was taking it upon himself to sort out my life, and for Minty, a nice young man was part of that fixing.

'My mates are great guys. Vetted.'

'Minty!'

He shrugs. 'This one you'd like.'

'You said that about the last one, and that was an all-out disaster.'

'Phil?'

I nod. 'Phil.'

'Phil's a great guy. On the right track, I'd have said.'

'Track?' I laugh. 'He took me trainspotting. That's not a date.'

'Well,' Minty shrinks down into his shoulders in a sheepish attitude, 'okay, so it's a bit of a specialised interest. But you know what, he's never late.'

'Then there was Darren.'

Minty breathes out sharply. 'Yeah, I don't know what went wrong there. Darren's a great bloke.'

'He told me my phone was running slow, so he downloaded new software. He fixed the gate on the front drive before he took me through it.'

'And he did a good job,' Minty says enthusiastically.

'Yeah, that was okay, but in the restaurant, he fixed the plumbing in the men's toilets.' I shoot Minty a hard stare. 'No one even asked him to do it.'

'Like I said,' Minty states with a sigh. 'Good bloke.'

'And then there was Kev cheap-at-half-the-price.'

'Kev can always spot a bargain.' Minty's voice is full of appreciation.

'But when he said take me out for a meal, I didn't realise he meant a supermarket meal deal.'

'Hmm.' Minty nods. 'You were a bit overdressed for that.'

'Yeah. It wasn't even a nice bench. So, I think I'll take a pass.' I flip open my bag and rummage for my phone. 'Why is it that as soon as a woman reaches twenty-five everybody thinks she should get herself hitched. I don't want a man.'

Only, of course I do, and of course, I'm lying. I gaze out of the window once again, thinking about what exactly I do want. I want a life like Evelyn's, which did have a starring role for a man in it. Only not my brother's friends. It had to be a man more like… like… An image flashes through my head: Marco Delagado. No way. I give myself a shake. I have got to get myself in check. The man is out of my league. Besides, he called me a goblin.

'How was choir practice last night?' Stan asks with a teasing grin, pushing his swing doors into a whirlwind for me to step into.

I press the disabled button, and the wide door next to the carousel slides open in front of me.

'No fun,' he says, raising one large bushy eyebrow as if still daring me to step into his revolving whirlpool and play.

'Absolutely no fun,' I confirm. 'Are there auditions again today?' I ask, sauntering towards my desk. Auditions seem to have been going on forever. They surely must have found their golden voice by now.

Stan follows me across the wide foyer. 'Just the tail end. Thank goodness we haven't had any tears yet. Usually, there are tears.'

Stan's words make me feel more than a little relieved I'd kept a lid on it yesterday during my please-ground-swallow-me-up moment. Stan's right – tears are a no-no in a place like Delagado Towers. Image is everything here. Emotions are not needed. Oblivious, Stan glances towards the lift, his eyebrows knitting as though perplexed. 'Odd thing is, though, no one's coming down from the studio.'

'Oh?' I'd only been working at the office for less than a year, so I'd never been here for one of their annual auditions. The talent trawl of Delagado Sounds. The Voice of the Nation is a national competition run by Delagado, sponsored by one of the terrestrial broadcasters. Sure, there are loads of these talent shows now, but this was the first, and a working record label runs it. The prize is totally sweet: a recording contract and studio backing. The event was legendary. I couldn't wait to see who they chose. Maybe it would be someone I had ushered through the door.

It wasn't actually part of my remit to get involved. I'm the receptionist for the entire building, not just the production company. Despite sharing a name, the main day-to-day running of the Towers and Delagado Design (the music side) doesn't really mix. The sound studio even has its own lift, but without a dedicated reception desk. So, most likely, they don't want the young hopefuls streaming in through that. The process goes on for around two weeks. It's relentless. If they go past the main reception, at least everything gets recorded. Besides, the main reception, with its high marble pillars, glass windows, and wide tongue of a reception area, is big-time swanky.

It's been so cool watching all the hopefuls traipsing by. Maybe I'm not involved with the glitz and the glamour going on in the studios above, but perhaps a little of that sparkle will rub off. What does it really matter if Marco Delagado caught me looking like a goblin? It's a well-known fact that he might be pretty, but the man has the personality of an ogre, so I guess that makes us quits, or maybe some kind of fairy-tale incompatible. Not sure ogres and goblins have ever been storyboarded as a match made in heaven.

I grab the clipboard from the hidden drawer beneath my desk (the drawer I had put in myself) and start unpacking lanyards. Stan's right, it looks like today is the drag end of the competition because there are only ten audition slots allocated.

'Is there a pile of lanyards from yesterday?' I say, glancing at my clipboard and the column of empty boxes where lanyards haven't been handed back in. Something's not stacking up here.

Stan shrugs. 'Like I said, I'm not sure anybody's come down. They ordered masses of food. Could be up there for the next twelve months.'

'That was yesterday,' I say, hoping Stan's not going to mention what I'm labelling in my head as 'the goblin incident'. Fortunately, he doesn't. But there's another problem. 'Hmm.' I chew on my bottom lip as I let the problem flit through my brain. 'I had people sign in yesterday, but very few signed out. This is going to be a mess. They must be using the other lift.'

'I guess,' Stan says, not really interested, idly giving the door another swing.

I sigh. When I first took this job in reception, I had hoped I'd be more involved in the audition process, not just meeting and greeting and badge disposal. It seems as though I'm outside of the glamour, and now it appears they're even using the other lift to avoid me. I can't help feeling a little bit disappointed.

'You didn't answer me about choir practice,' Stan says casually. 'Did you get a chance to exercise your inner diva?'

I shrug, trying to play it cool despite the buzz of warmth I can still feel glowing inside me from last night. 'It was fine.'

'Hmm.' He raises a bushy, sceptical eyebrow. 'Something happened.'

I shrug. 'It was just practice. Normal.'

He shakes his head slowly. 'Clara, I can tell when you're sitting on something, girl. Spill.'

'Okay, okay.' I glance around, making sure we're alone, before whispering, 'I had a solo.'

'A solo!' Stan's eyes light up. 'That's wonderful! See,' he says, moving across the marble hall towards me. 'I told you that you were ready.'

'It was just for one hymn,' I say, feeling my cheeks flush. 'But... it went well. Evelyn, the choirmaster, said I was a natural.'

Stan's grinning from ear to ear. The man couldn't look prouder if I'd just told him I'd saved the world from an impending collision with a meteor.

'A natural talent like you,' he says, slapping me gently on the back, 'belongs on an actual stage, not stuck behind this reception desk.' He leans in conspiratorially. 'You should try out for the auditions.' He points with one finger towards the ceiling. 'Absolutely, you should, Clara. Tell you what,' his eyes spark with the glint of an idea, 'I'll call the lift.'

For one moment, the world seems to slow. Maybe Stan's right. Maybe I could do this. I glance over towards the golden bank of elevators. It's just one push of a button. Just one ride up to the top floor. An unused lanyard tangles around my fingers. I could do this. I could.

But before I get a chance to respond or take one tiny step forward to my dreams, the lift doors start to open. My face drops. Stan and I both hear it at the exact same time: gasps and chokes and tears.

'Oh, ugh, what did I tell you,' Stan mumbles. 'There are always broken dreams and waterfalls of weeping.'

I drop the unused lanyard back into the box. Well, the tears have certainly put me off auditioning. I'm terrified of singing solo at the best of times. No way could I put myself through an audition process. No doubt the tears were provoked by that ogre of a man, Marco. He'll have taken his insults just a step too far. I feel the bile rising inside me. I would so love to give that entitled, arrogant idiot a piece of my…

There's another loud sob before, suddenly, a young woman comes hurtling out of the lift, mascara streaked down her cheeks. A snotty tissue clutched tightly in her manicured hands. Instinctively, I take a step towards her, only… I stop, my mind re-processing the situation. Something's not right. Confused, I glance down at my list. Amy. The woman's name is Amy. I know her, but she can't be auditioning. Amy is Marco Delagado's PA.

My eyes widen in alarm. 'Amy, what's wrong?'

She just shakes her head and keeps on running.

I glance at Stan, who nods. 'Go on, see if she's all right. I'll watch the desk. I get the feeling a woman's touch is what's needed.'

'Thanks, Stan.'

Once outside, I pause for a moment, listening. A water feature can be heard burbling, and despite the fact this is the city, you can hear the faint rustle of carefully curated trees willowing in the light breeze. I walk over to the mesh of wooden paths, wondering which direction Amy might have taken. It doesn't take long to find her crumpled on a marble bench beneath a curiously serene and indifferent cherry blossom. The poor woman is sobbing into her hands, at total odds with the landscape, the haven of willow tall grasses, flowers, and trees. This place has had mindfulness and serenity built into the design brief. In contrast, poor Amy looks like she's had the life pulled out of her.

'Amy.' I sit down beside her, placing one arm gently around her shoulders. I pull a clean tissue from my pocket and press it into her open palm. 'What's wrong? What happened?'

She hiccups before blowing her nose. 'Marco. Marco Delagado, he sacked me,' she says miserably. 'Just like that. After everything I've done for him, all the late nights I've put in, the weekends I've given up. The friends I've cancelled on. That man fired me...' She gulps, almost too choked to talk. 'He fired me in the middle of the studio. In front of everyone.' She sobs again.

'Oh no,' I say sympathetically, pushing a strand of hair gently away from her face. Marco Delagado. He's usually the figure in the papers with his hand over his face. Yesterday was the first time I'd actually seen what he looked like, and okay, so he was pretty, but seriously, this man is a monster. He's known for his brilliance on the music production front and his eccentricity in equal measure. But it's not exactly a well-kept secret that there's also a volatile temper in the mix, an impatience that can run nought to sixty if even the slightest mistake is made.

'I'm so sorry,' I say. 'Maybe he didn't mean it. He's probably just stressed about the auditions. Once he calms down, he'll realise he can't do without you.'

Amy had arrived in the building at the same time as me, just under twelve months ago. Unlike Marco, she fraternised with the workers on the lower levels. I liked her. She would always stop by my desk every morning for a debrief. Sometimes, she even came bearing croissants. How could you not like someone who did that? 'Just give it a bit of time,' I say reassuringly. 'Wait till that temper cools, and I know he'll be begging you to come back. You do a fantastic job. They'll be lost without you.'

Amy shakes her head. 'You don't understand. Lately, he's been impossible to please. Yelling at everyone, changing his mind every five minutes. I think...' she lowers her voice, '...he's been drinking. Hitting the bottle during the auditions.'

I'd seen him with a bottle only yesterday, but I hadn't realised it was a regular thing. It seems so disrespectful; if the artists are giving it their best shot Marco Delagado ought to have the courtesy to give exactly the same back.

'And...' Amy sobs. 'His awful ex is always hanging around.'

Oh dear, I think. 'Nobody needs an awful ex.'

'Exactly.' Amy nods, blowing her nose again. 'And now that I've gone, there's no one left to hold everything together. It's going to be a total disaster. All those young women, he just doesn't realise.' She looks at me with imploring blue eyes. 'This is their dream.'

Hmm, none of this seems fair. Marco Delagado may be a musical genius, but he needs someone to keep him in line and make sure these auditions happen. If only for the girls involved. He's going to be lost without Amy. The whole thing could go belly-up.

Suddenly, poor Amy starts frantically clutching at her sides. Patting herself down as though she's on fire. A look of pure panic whitening her already pale features. 'Oh no, I don't believe it,' she gasps.

'What?'

She glances towards me, her eyes about to brim over again. 'I've forgotten my bag. The green Gucci one with the gold clasp.'

I knew the bag well; she'd picked it up at TK Maxx only two weeks ago. She was so proud of it. The damn thing cost her a month's wages.

'I left in such a hurry.' In utter despair, Amy drags her hands through her short, bobbed hair. 'I can't go back up there. I can't. I just…'

'Don't worry, Amy. I'll go. You get yourself home, I'll retrieve the bag, and have it biked over to you.'

She sniffs, thankfully. 'You're an angel, Clara.'

'I'm not sure about that.' I'm a receptionist, pure and simple, but that won't stop me from trying to sort this. 'I'll get that bag back to you.'

I stand, brush my hands across my smart, blue work skirt, trying to build up courage. Marco Delagado sounds truly terrifying, and what if he recognises me from yesterday? A million hideous scenarios dance through my brain. Say he laughs at me?

'Are you okay?' Amy asks through her tears.

'Fine,' I say, drawing myself up. 'Absolutely fine.'

CHAPTER 4

CLARA

'Don't worry,' Stan says, walking me to the lift. 'I'll hold the fort here.'

'Amy's in a terrible state.'

'Hmm.' He draws in his thin lips. 'Not surprising. I hate being sacked.'

I glance at him curiously. 'How many times have you been sacked?'

He takes a deep breath. 'Another story, Clara. This one's not mine. You get yourself up to that top floor and get it sorted. Only…' He reaches out and presses the golden button. The call light goes on. The lift is currently all the way up on the seventeenth floor. 'Only maybe…' Stan clears his throat. 'Don't get yourself sacked as well, eh?'

'Not helpful.'

He laughs. But I can't find it in me. This is not funny. In fact, I wish Stan would just keep it buttoned for a bit.

I can't believe I'm standing waiting for the golden lift. Not quite in the way I dreamed of yesterday, but even though this is just a mercy mission, I have to admit that my knees are feeling more than a little weak. The smallest puff of wind could knock me over like a bowling pin. Let's hope that monster of a man doesn't bellow at me.

'I'll just get in and get back out again really quickly,' I say more to myself than Stan as the lift doors draw back.

'Going up,' Stan says with a wink as I step into the mirrored cage.

'Oh dear.' I do not want to be doing this. 'I look such a mess,' I say, glancing at my image in the reflected mirrors and rubbing a trace of mascara from under my eyes. Well, maybe not a total mess, but certainly not like the people who inhabit the seventeenth floor.

Stan smirks. 'You can wear the mask if it'll make you feel more comfortable.'

I turn back towards him. The man is grinning like a Cheshire Cat.

'Told you you were going places.'

'Not funny,' I say.

Stan laughs. 'Try this.' And he pretends to get his face stuck in the lift. The last image I see before the doors finally slide shut is a rectangle of reception with Stan's wrinkled face, squeezing back out of the gap in the doors. The man is a health and safety liability.

I count the floors as the lift ascends, hoping someone from one of the other companies in the building might get in, might give me a smile, might say something regular and everyday, like talk about the weather. But no one gets in. When the lift doors finally slide back, I get the distinct feeling that, never mind Stan's brain, it's my legs which have jellified. I may be on the seventeenth floor. It may look as swanky as a hotel, but the place is mayhem. I get the feeling that even if I had been wearing the goblin mask, nobody would have noticed. There's a man with a whole seventies thing going on: the hair, the flares, the glasses, and he's chasing a shrieking woman who's dressed as a horse. I let the lift doors close without getting out. I seriously can't do this. But then I think of poor Amy, and I know I have to. When the lift doors open again, it's a whole different scenario. A gaggle of dolled-up singers with the most perfect hairdos on the planet, dressed in sequins and pearls, are milling about, arms woven together as neat as corn dolls, chatting like true sisters. Sadly, one trips over the slumped horse woman, who appears to now be flat-out on the floor.

No, I seriously can't do this. The doors start to close again. It's then that I see Amy's handbag. The green Gucci one with the gold clasp. Whatever the personal cost, I've got to get that bag back.

I step out onto the carpet of chaos. Somewhere, loud music is pumping. Not the melodic kind, but the kind guaranteed to drive anyone slowly but surely towards insanity. I push past two large women arguing about their proposed singing order. Somebody punches somebody else. Then there's a kind of combined hair-pulling involving a significant loss of hairpieces and extensions. I duck out of the way, clutching my curls, and narrowly avoid the path of a bald man with a long goatee who is accusing a girl, who looks like she's just stepped out of a *Mamma Mia* hologram, of stealing his vocals. I'm not sure how this is possible since they are all supposed to be singing cover songs, but I don't wish to get involved.

There are child-sized unopened snack baskets, abandoned platters of sushi, something nasty happening with what I so hope is wasabi, and a multitude of half-consumed water bottles littered across a low-slung series of red leather couches. Above them is what can only be described as a red wine calamity spewed across the entirety of one once-white wall. I wonder if it's art, then again, on closer inspection, the thing is still dripping, so that would seem unlikely.

In short, it's all bad. All very bad, and standing there in the middle of the floor, waving his arms like a windmill with a screw loose, shouting vacuously in each and every direction, is the tall, thin, wavy-haired piece of hunk I met yesterday. Only now, he's not looking quite so fresh. His brown eyes have lost that deep chestnut depth, switched up in favour of bloodshot spider's webs. His hair is mussed rather than wavy, and his lips are stained in a dried scarlet kiss-of-death alcohol bruise. No wonder he keeps his hand over his face when the paparazzi are after him. If he drinks this much normally, I can see why he'd be shy. My mask could even come in handy. I should let him borrow it.

I stand there, looking aghast. This whole place has gone to pot. It's such a contrast from the serenity of the marble hall downstairs, and it's so not what I thought the seventeenth floor would be like. I mean, sure, there's partying and fun, but this does not look like anyone's idea of a fun party. Slowly, I step towards the Gucci bag, which is resting on a glass coffee table. The thing looks so out of place. Like Cinderella's glass slipper displayed on a podium. An item of magical perfection from a different realm. I'm almost there; it's practically within reach when an empty whisky bottle rolls under one of the couches, coming to rest against my foot.

There are four women and six men in tears. Each one clutching sheet music to their heaving chests. They're not even standing together in their grief. Everyone is trapped in their own private hell of failure. It's no way to treat people. Marco Delagado might be rich, he might be brilliant, he might even be great-looking when not intoxicated, but the man is totally out of order. Luckily, I'm used to just about every flavour of bad behaviour that it's possible to exhibit. I have my brother, Minty, and his mates to thank for that. Since I was twelve, I have spent my life having to step over and sort out. Replace the empty bottles for machine parts, remove the distraught 'artists', and this present shambles is not a million miles from my world.

I scoop up the whisky bottle and stride over to Marco, interrupting whatever nonsense it is that he happens to be spouting. It sounds like a lot of name-dropping with a few well-placed Ringos and at least one Sheeran in the mix.

'Mr Delagado,' I say coolly. 'I'm here to assist you for the day.'

Before I've even managed to wrangle down my mind and work out why I've said it, Marco Delagado whirls around looking gorgeous, intense, and, it has to be admitted, totally out of control. He's spluttering with rage, one arm actually drawing back as if to push me away, but then the oddest thing happens. The entire room seems to take a deep intake of breath as if the world is running slower. His brown eyes glint through the cracks of red. His head lollops to one side. Everything stills, and his anger melts. His features soften. Even in this state, he's clearly a good-looking man. I'll give him that. In fact, he's just my type: cheeky attitude, chiselled face, and gorgeous muscle-toned arms. But everything about him says bad news. He's the sort of bad news my brother would have a problem with. It wouldn't matter if he owned the country. My brother would not be impressed by that. Minty is only ever impressed by what he calls 'great blokes'. People like him and his friends. People who treat women right – treat them like their princesses. That's why the dating thing has been a problem. Minty and I have a very different idea as to who I should be dating, and sometimes, it's just easier to go with the flow. But I'm not doing that anymore. No more meal deals, fixed gates, or trainspotting. I have to find my own Mr Right, and this is clearly not the place to be doing that. Currently, I'm fully expecting an earful of abuse. But this is not about my brother and his plans for me. This is the here and now and instead of giving me a mouthful, Marco Delagado drinks me in, looks into my eyes in an oddly curious way, like a scientist peering down a microscope.

'And who would you be, my little darling?' His voice, despite the slur and the appalling brewery breath and patronising choice of words, has a velvet tone.

It's the kind of tone that should make a woman feel special, even when he's swaying, and I can't help wondering how many women have fallen for it. But I know better. Beneath the charm is a careless cruelty. I saw what he did to Amy.

I tilt my chin up, meeting his gaze straight from the barrel. 'I'm not your darling, sweetheart,' I say, drawing myself up to my full five foot six. 'I'm Clara Thompson, and I'm here to make sure your auditions run on schedule.'

There's another one of those pauses. Only now, it's packed with tension. I wonder if he's going to start shouting. I also wonder what the hell I'm doing. I had only taken the elevator up here to retrieve a bag, but somehow, when I saw so many people having their dreams crushed, it just made me mad.

'You…' he slurs, pointing towards my chest. 'And you…' The finger remains extended, but suddenly he shrugs, turning away, already dismissing me. 'Do as you like.' Marco waves one hand wildly through the air. 'Just make sure I have talent in front of me within the hour, or you'll both be out of jobs.'

I don't bother to tell him that there's only one of me. It doesn't seem like the time to be pedantic. Instead, I take a deep breath and turn to face the crowd of disgruntled artists, clapping my hands sharply for their attention.

'Okay, everyone, let's get started!' I say, pitching my voice so that it carries. 'The auditions will begin in thirty minutes. Please sign in and then warm up your voices. Let's make some music!' I'm beginning to sound like Evelyn.

A ripple of excitement moves through the group. Marco snorts and collapses onto the couch, grabbing a handful of cashews. I ignore him, moving to the sign-in table and straightening the stacks of paperwork. The penthouse studio is a mess, and Marco Delagado is a menace. But if I can pull this off, it might just be my big break. Okay, so maybe I don't get to be on the mic side of the action, but this, for all its crisis and colour, is the music business. I smile, ready to face the challenge.

CHAPTER 5

MARCO

Another day. Morning already. It's light outside, and I can hear the lift shaft's constant whir, so I guess the workers in the Tower must be arriving. Arriving! Lucky buggers. We didn't even get to leave last night. This whole process is proving to be chaos. All of those people throughout the building, managing to clock in, clock out. But not here. Not on the seventeenth floor. Not in the music business. If just one person could manage to do their job properly, I swear I'd give them the keys to the kingdom. Nobody has had enough sleep, and everyone is irritating. By that, I mean even more irritating than normal. Terry, on keyboard, keeps saying 'star quality'. He says it about everyone. It is so clearly not true. The sound these singers are making is not even in the same region as heavenly. Not even orbiting. Not even out of the gravitational pull of piss poor. This is making me think Terry must have something else feeding into his headphones. Or maybe he's just lost his marbles, or his hearing. It's possible. He never gets emotional, and I swear his piano's out of tune. Okay, so it's electronic, but he's playing it flat. Then there's Jeff. What the hell is up with Jeff? He seems unable to get the right sound mix. Luckily, I'm here to keep him in line. Even so, the musicians aren't the key problem – are they ever? It's the starlets, they would sound better if they sang through their noses. Sadly, that is no word of a lie. I've had two hours' sleep. Maybe less. So, yes, my temper is running a bit short, but there is nada wrong with my hearing. And then Amy, my assistant. If she hands me one more glass of water, I swear, she'll get it thrown over her. I'm not a fish. I don't need water. I do not need to hydrate. I don't have time because today is the last day of auditions. That's why we worked through the night. I took that decision. This evening I'll have to do the announcement in front of the Tower. Standing next to the dewy-eyed hopeful that I'm about to jettison into the fame stratosphere. So no, I do not have time for anything apart from finding that voice. But all I hear every time anyone steps into the booth is some sub-standard regurgitation of somebody else's sound.

'I need another drink,' I call out to that no-good Amy, rolling an empty whisky bottle away from my feet.

'I'm not sure that's a good idea,' she says, which is kind of funny because I was not asking her if she thought it was a good idea.

'Yeah, well, thanks for the input, Amy, but no thanks. Get me another bottle. Then line up the next embarrassment of riches.'

Amy's looking flustered. When she talks again, her voice is lower. I barely get one word of what she's saying. 'Don't mumble.'

She looks embarrassed, hisses back, 'They can hear you.'

I glance around. Does she think that I care? 'Where's the new sound?' I say, wringing my hands in frustration. 'Give me something from the soul.'

'Sure.' Some kid with braids steps forward. 'I can do that, sir.'

'Me too.' It's the girl with the horse's head. What's she still even doing here?

'I'm all soul,' says some blonde who looks like Marilyn Monroe, only a cheap version. The kind you might get out of a Christmas cracker – if a Christmas cracker was big enough. I swear, if the woman sings 'My Heart Belongs to Daddy' one more time. And what is it with the breathiness? Why is everyone breathing down the mic every time they get close? 'Where's the voice, for Christ's sake? The voice!'

Amy's tugging at my arm gently. Gently, but it's still a tug.

'Get your hands–'

'Maybe we should take a day off. Come back tomorrow?'

I pull away. 'Seriously, honey.' I fix her with my eyes. I can tell they've gone flint-like, and so I have to carry it through. 'Tomorrow is going to be difficult because you, you, Amy, are fired today.'

There's a gasp in the room, then absolute and utter silence, which is great because all I want is silence. But it doesn't last because then comes the sob. The Amy girl is wilting, or melting, or whatever else unattractive thing she happens to be doing, and off she goes, running for the door. 'Great,' I say, calling after her. 'And don't bother coming back.'

After that, things get a bit cloudy. Or maybe it would be better to call it raucous. I kind of envy Amy. I wish I'd taken the lift down. People are pestering the hell out of me with questions. The schedule seems to have slipped out of control. I'm about to tell them what a talentless bunch of imbeciles they all are when suddenly I turn around, and there's this woman behind me. She can't have been there for long. She looks like she's slept. She's not like the others. She has this golden hair hanging over her shoulders, I mean a lot of hair, wavy stuff, and a body to die for. She kind of looks familiar. Kind of, almost. The world seems to still, and the wonderful thing is, there are two of these creatures. I close one eye, no, it's one. I open both eyes. No, two of them. I scrunch one eye again – definitely one.

'And who would you be, my little darling?' I always use the word 'darling' if I'm feeling out of kilter. It's got a lovely echo of superiority that might just give me an edge, seeing as I'm so desperate not to slur. And I am hoping against hope that this beauty has come to audition. But when she looks back at me, there's no deference there, which is odd. I'm used to deference. I get it all the time, but with her, there's none of that. Instead, she lifts her chin and meets my gaze straight on.

'I'm not your darling, sweetheart,' she says.

Seriously, she called me sweetheart! Which, I have to admit, tops it hands down on the patronising scale.

'I'm Clara.'

I like the name. It's got that clean, fresh ring to it. It suits her.

'And I'm here to make sure your auditions run on schedule.'

I have to fight really hard not to smile. Part of me just wants to burst out laughing. This pint-sized – okay, so she's attractive – but this pint-sized, attractive ball of energy has just slam-dunked me with a hardcore dose of my own slice of good old-fashioned passive-aggressiveness. Suddenly, I realise there's a pause going on. People are watching. I'm no longer in control.

'You…' I say, managing not to slur, pointing towards her chest. 'You…' And what I'd like to say is, you can just run away with me. Take that hard-boiled attitude, drop it in the bin on the way out, and fly off with me to some place with bucketloads of sunshine-infused paradise. The thought of that blonde vision in blue, in a bikini, with her soft skin under a warm sun starts circulating around my brain. Suddenly, I realise I've been standing there swaying, with the full attention of all those star-struck hopefuls who didn't make it out of the studio last night. Oh dear. This has all gone badly wrong. It feels like I'm way down deep in a black hole and have no idea how to pull myself out. 'You do as you like.' I say – which seems like the safest bet. 'Just,' again there's a pause, everybody hanging off my every word, 'make sure I have talent in front of me within the hour, or…' I squint. Why are there two of them? 'Or you'll both be out of a job.'

With that, she claps her hands sharply for attention.

It was that easy. That easy for this, whoever she is, to lick them all into shape. I sink back onto the red couch, grabbing a handful of nuts and a bottle of water. It's been a tough night. Why did the auditions carry on right through the clock? Hmm, was that a case of me being an arsehole? Maybe. Thank Christ, the fireball with the clapping hands has finally got it under control. The goblin woman, I mutter to myself as I fall asleep, tugging at the edges of my brain. Of course! I laugh. She's a goblin. Then everything goes velvet-black.

CHAPTER 6

CLARA

It's such a relief when Marco flops backwards on the sofa, closes his eyes, and snores. This is a mess. I'm not even one hundred per cent sure that I can clear the clutter, but I need to make a start. First things first, I need to dismiss the hangers-on, the ones still milling about the studio from yesterday. They haven't found their way home, despite the fact they're not wanted, so they're taking up space and distracting from the actual work. Not to mention they're beginning to smell! Party animals have an eight-hour shelf life.

I can see, from what must be Amy's clipboard on the glossy white reception desk, who auditioned yesterday. Thankfully, Amy stuck badges on them as well as the lanyards, so I can tally the names up with what I'm guessing must be Amy's notes on their audition. She's clearly working to a code. CB must mean call-back. LG, let go? And I'm guessing NW is probably something like no way. I can make this work. I check I have all the audition tracks for the artists I'm about to send home and that their contact details match up, just in case, before pressing a bottle of water into each clammy, dismissed, sleep-deprived hand and showing them the lift.

With the space cleared, I can focus on setting up for the day's auditions. Today's cohort is already streaming in and looking as confused as I feel. I need to pull this process around. It's a disaster.

A long, skinny woman with an aquiline nose gives Marco's sleeping foot a stroke. 'You'll have to wake him when I do my slot,' she says, without taking her eyes from him.

I gaze down at the snoring Marco; there is no way I'm going to poke that beast. If he's asleep, he's staying that way. 'I'm so sorry,' I say, 'but he's not feeling too good.'

This is not a lie. The man was most definitely unsteady, slurring, and most likely seeing double. In short, useless. 'He won't be awake for any of the auditions,' I say gently, keen to get the disappointment over with as quickly as possible. There are murmurs of frustration.

A woman with a tattooed face and a diamond nose ring frowns. 'But I shine when I sing.'

It must be through some kind of halo accessory because there's no way any sort of natural flush is getting through that skin. But that's not my business.

'I'm sure,' I say, sympathetically. 'Don't worry. I'll set up cameras. We have all the best kit.'

I have no idea if that's true or not, but the last thing I need is a mutiny on my hands.

'Is it 4K?' asks a blonde who looks like Marilyn.

'Six,' I say neatly, hoping that the technology I'm alluding to has been invented and is suitably impressive. From the girl's reaction, it seems I've hit at least one of my marks, possibly both.

'Just don't grade me blue,' Marilyn preens.

I press one hand to my chest in an attitude that says absolute sincerity. 'I wouldn't do that, ever.'

She nods.

I'm getting carried away now and have no idea what I'm on about or if I'm even making sense. Luckily, someone claps at this point. I make a mental note to find out what the hell 'grade' means.

'Okay,' I say brightly, with as much energy as I can muster. 'If you can just give me some space. Help yourself to refreshments, and we'll be rolling soon.'

The crowd disperses. People start stretching their bodies into artistic shapes, contorted postures that I didn't even know were possible. Personally, I just uncross my fingers. Whatever I did seems to have worked.

❧

After placing Amy's bag in a locked cupboard, I text Stan, who's in the lobby, urging him to get cover for the day. This is not going to be tied up anytime soon. Then I do a super swift room tidy before I go through the call sheets, noting the names of the production staff. I make sure they have everything they need for the next raft of auditions. At the sound deck, I have a beanie-wearing technician called Jeff. He has a lot of facial hair and carries with him the curious smell of damp towels. I'm not sure if that's because of the late night they've all had or because that's just Jeff. Either way, he's friendly enough, and in my book, friendly works. He's also efficient, so, wet towels or not, he's getting full marks. He's collected all the recordings from the previous day's auditions. Everything is ready for mixing and a light edit. I don't know how this competition works, but I do know I need to ensure the judges have high-quality recordings to review. Some of the contestants have travelled miles, and I can't let them down.

After a pretty frantic hour, I glance around the studio, checking everything's in place. The space is uncluttered. Jeff and Terry, the keyboard player, have set the equipment up in the studio, and the contestants are ready and waiting. Everything seems in order. I can't help but feel a surge of satisfaction at how

I've pulled the situation around. What will the great Marco Delagado think when he comes to? Maybe he'll give me a permanent job. Perhaps this is just the push I need.

I look over at Terry, a sweet-looking guy in a white shirt and waistcoat. He's sitting at the piano in the recording studio, idly playing a few notes.

'Terry, are we all set? Do you have all the music for the auditions?' I ask, peering around the door.

He nods, his fingers dancing across the keys. 'Yep, all tuned and ready to go. It's actually electric, so–'

'No tuning,' I say.

He points at me, 'you-got-it' style. 'And the acoustics are always perfect in here.' He glances admiringly around at the studio. 'You have to say that about Marco. For all the chaos, everything he owns is quality.'

Luckily, I managed to locate the camera, which is in a flight case. It doesn't take me long to fix it on a tripod, positioning it for optimal view of the stage area. The angle looks great. I may have to adjust for height, but I'm pretty sure I've got most scenarios covered. I hook it up to a monitor and turn it on to test the feed. The red light blinks, signalling it's recording. This is nothing that I haven't done before with my brother for his TikTok page. He sells bits of old cars on social media platforms. It sometimes amazes me how many ways there are to make a living. Then again, my brother never did fit into the school career path model. He just followed his interest, his passion, and everything worked out all right.

Soon, the studio is prepped and the equipment primed. Stan sent up a team from housekeeping to deep clean the parts of the office that I hadn't got to, so we are at least looking presentable. Although I'm not sure the red wine stain is coming off the wall anytime soon. But that can't be my worry. My main focus has to be the auditions. The contestants all have their cues and know the approximate time they'll be called for their slot. Some have even managed to nip out for a coffee. Sticking to a tight schedule is best for everyone. I survey the room with a satisfied smile. If Marco Delagado ever wakes up, he is surely going to be impressed with how I've taken charge of the situation. Or so I think. Unfortunately, it's just then that Marco pulls himself, bleary-eyed, up from the couch. He yawns loudly and scratches his head, before glancing around in total confusion.

He blinks at me, dazed. 'The auditions. Right?' Marco shakes his head as though trying to clear the cobwebs. 'Who are you?'

'Clara.' I feel my confidence draining away.

'Great,' he says, pulling one large, tanned hand through his thick hair. 'Well…' He looks at me appraisingly, as if realising the whole turnaround is down to me and seems pretty impressed. I think he's going to say something. A thanks would be nice, but instead, he just nods. 'Okay… and yeah… yeah, let's get this show on the road.'

The contestants clap. A genuine show of approval, and despite the fact he has been sound asleep on the sofa, Marco basks in it, turning side to side, smiling, drinking it up. Very sweetly, a few of the braver souls shoot me kind looks. I may be the unsung hero, but I know what they're thinking – without me, this entire day would have been a total disaster.

'Hey.' Marco looks at me, those brown eyes so sincere, so inviting. And for an intense moment, I just know he's going to say something, congratulate me on pulling it all into shape. He smiles.

'Clara.' I nod eagerly offering my name once again.

'Clara,' he repeats. 'Since everything is under control here, can you run yourself out to get some breakfast sandwiches?'

My heart sinks. Despite all I've done, I'm still just the skivvy.

'I didn't have time to eat this morning,' he adds in explanation.

I try to smile, honestly, I do, but this feels like a total slap in the face. The man has zero manners. My brother is so right. Bad boys are not all they're cracked up to be. This particular specimen would be a nightmare to date. I'm about to give him a mouthful when an icy voice cuts through my thoughts.

'Well, isn't this cosy?'

I turn to find a woman in her late forties peering at us with narrowed eyes. She's impeccably dressed in designer clothes and heels, her auburn hair swept into a sleek chignon. Everything about her screams wealth and status so loudly that I feel like I might come down with tinnitus. My smile falters. Suddenly, I feel ridiculously underdressed, even though I'm wearing my best peacock-blue wrap dress. I have no idea who this woman is, but I can already tell she doesn't like me.

'Betsy,' Marco says, getting to his feet.

Betsy… Betsy. I scan my brain. Of course, this must be Betsy Miller. Marco's business partner. I've only ever seen pictures of the woman, her stern face staring out from our website.

'I thought you didn't come in on Fridays?' Marco yawns.

Unsurprisingly, the man is suffering from a serious case of whisky breath.

Betsy crinkles her large, flat nose. 'It's the auditions. Last day. The biggest vocal contest in the country. Sod Fridays.' She shakes her immaculately coifed head, irritated. 'You know, Marco.' She sniffs. 'Has anyone ever told you, you stink?'

'Frequently.' He laughs. 'Betsy, this is…' He waves his arm towards me.

'Clara,' I say helpfully.

'Clara,' he repeats, 'she works here now.'

'I don't, not officially,' I find myself stuttering. This woman makes me feel like a child. 'Actually, I work on reception downstairs.'

'Oh, that's it!' a sweet redhead says. 'Now I remember. I saw her yesterday at the desk. She was very helpful. Pointed me in the direction of the lifts. Gave me a lanyard.' She fiddles with the card around her neck as if to demonstrate.

'Well, now.' Marco flashes his wild, energetic eyes around the room, stopping when they get to me, causing my heart to somersault. 'Now she works here.'

'That's not how it goes, Marco,' Betsy says, shaking her head. Enjoying the negative motion just a little bit too much. 'She's–'

'Clara,' Marco interrupts.

I'm surprised. He's taking it all in.

'Clara,' Betsy corrects herself, 'works on the main desk reception. You can't go poaching people just because they bring you a latte.'

'She didn't. She hasn't got to that yet,' Marco snaps back.

Hmm. I'm not so keen on the attitude.

'Besides, she's not on reception anymore. Now she works for me, full-time, here.'

Betsy's lips curl into a frigid smile. 'And Amy?'

Marco waves his hand dismissively like an irritated fly is buzzing around his face. 'Amy, that was a different job description. That was yesterday.'

I clear my throat, determined not to let Betsy intimidate me. I would love this job, but I don't want to tread on Amy's toes.

'This is not just organisational PA stuff, Amy stuff. I need someone to help more with the music production.'

Working around musicians would be a dream come true. I have to be the bigger person here. 'So pleased to meet you, Betsy.'

The woman's eyes narrow further. Why do I feel like such an imposter? I feel sure she's going to bark me out of the room. Throw me down the lift shaft. But her features soften just a little when I extend my hand out for a shake, even if she doesn't take it. She must be able to see that everything is under control here. I clearly have my uses.

'Just make sure you log everything,' she says. 'You'll find my notes on Amy's desk about how I like it all formatted. No mistakes. I want it by tomorrow.'

'Not a problem.' I smile, but behind my back I have my fingers crossed. It's not just Marco that I need to please in order to land this job.

❧

MARCO

When I come to, my mouth is really dry. The kind of dry that feels as though you've been munching on sawdust all night or licking a deep shag carpet. Sadly, I'm not in bed. I'm in a public space, on the red couch in my studio. I've never seen so many people milling around, including a lot of seriously over-made-up women in skimpy clothes with odd hairdos. One good thing, they all look happy. They're smiling, which was not the situation when I passed out. The nice-looking woman in blue is still here. I think this is a good thing. She's ushering people into order, and she seems to know a lot about music. I like her.

'The auditions,' I mumble, wiping a trail of dribble from the corner of my mouth. Shit, I'm a mess. 'Right!' I roar, giving my head a quick shake before flexing my bones. Things start cracking. I'm not going to let on, but I'm seriously too old to be sleeping on couches. Far too old. 'Remind me?' I say, squinting my eyes at the woman I met just before I went under.

'Clara,' the woman in blue says, the one with the glorious body and skeins of gold flowing over her shoulders.

Stop this, I think. I need to get myself under control. No affairs at work. That's my mantra. I feel myself frowning, stumbling over the loophole. Does she actually work for me, though? Interesting. It's then that I realise I haven't said anything for a while and she's looking straight at me. Intently.

'Great.' I pull a hand through my hair. I need to go to the bathroom. Freshen up. Thankfully, I keep a wash bag in my office. I might not have affairs with people in the building, but I sometimes bring them back here. Music and women – it's always a turn-on. Wait. What am I thinking? This is our biggest time of the year. The auditions. Why am I getting sidetracked by this woman? I glance around again. It's not just the fact that everyone is smiling now, I seem to remember when I went to sleep this place was chaos; now it looks, well, kind of normal. I stare back at this Clara woman. Did she do all this? On her own? How does that even work? She must have an entourage hidden somewhere. Everybody does these days.

'Well, yeah… Let's get this show on the road.'

At this, there's a lot of clapping. I enjoy clapping. Who doesn't enjoy clapping? But I try not to bask in it too long. We've have got serious work to do. I'm guessing we're behind. 'Hey, Clara?'

She's smiling up at me, all wide-eyed. So happy, so gorgeous, so… I'd like to take her into my arms and run my fingers through that hair, touch that face, slide my hands across her… Audition! I think. I've wasted enough time.

'Clara,' I repeat. Best get her at a safe distance. She nods again at the sound of her name. I'm starving and I can't leave this mess, so I ask her kindly if she could go out and grab breakfast.

Her face falls a little, like she was expecting something else. I'm not sure what, but it's not as if I'm asking her to pay. I reach in my pocket for some money, my company card. Only then, guess what? The true goblin arrives. The one that doesn't need a mask. Betsy Miller, my partner. The partner I had to get into bed with, not literally, be thankful for small mercies. But let's just say the music business is not what it used to be. Betsy came in with the dosh, but there's no such thing as a free tune. She has hoops she's keen to make me jump through.

'Well, isn't this cosy?' My partner leers.

I'd thought she wasn't going to come in for the auditions. We've been at it for so long. I had hoped she was getting bored, and I know for a fact she doesn't like working on a Friday. Betsy is the money side of the equation, not the creative side, and for me, those two things don't mix.

I introduce her to the new girl. Betsy gives the poor young woman in blue a withering gaze.

'Clara works here now,' I say. I'm sure as hell not letting her go. Even if I have to write her out on the romance front. I'm not questioning how she pulled things together; I just know that she did, and I need that in my life more than I need sex. I can get sex. When you have a recording studio with gold records on the wall and a sports car, sex is simple. Besides, there's Fitz. Why do I always forget about Fitz? We're supposed to be engaged. Kind of. Shouldn't Fitz be taking up more of my brain, more of my bed. I can't remember the last time…

But the thought gets shut down *tout de suite* by Betsy, who launches into this whole lecture on how I shouldn't be poaching people from other departments.

I don't care. I'll poach exactly who I want when I want.

'Sorry, Betsy,' I say, holding up one hand. 'We were just in the middle of something here. Like national auditions.' I turn my attention back to Clara. She looks up at me again with those baby blue eyes that you just want to sink into. 'Bacon bap, with ketchup, and a black Americano,' I say before returning my focus to the room. 'People, we have work to do.' And I clap my hands, just like Clara did yesterday, or was it this morning? Time seems to be going off-piste. Never mind. It doesn't matter because everyone nods excitedly. That clapping shit, it really works.

CHAPTER 7

CLARA

The office is eerily empty. The only sound is the tapping of my fingers on the keyboard. I glance at the clock – it's already after 7pm. My stomach grumbles in protest. I should take a break, but I've still got two more sheets of hopeful candidates to log.

I sigh and save the file I've been working on for the past few hours. Pushing back my chair, I give my aching body a good stretch. By tomorrow, all the auditions will be logged for Betsy in just the way she wants it. Everything will be saved to the flash drive she gave me and entered in the exact format she'd asked for. I'm determined to win the woman over. I've been professional all my working life, even if I have been working in the wrong profession. This is my chance, and once Marco is on more of an even keel, I'll get Amy back in here too. There's enough work for both of us.

Terry pokes his head into the office. 'You're still here, Clara? Jeff and I are heading to Luigi's for pasta and wine. You should join us.'

I force a smile. 'Thanks, but I have to finish up. You guys go on ahead.'

Terry smirks. 'Where have you been all our lives? Did you manage to weasel out of your other job?'

'Hmm.' I raise one eyebrow thoughtfully. 'Not so keen on the word weasel.' I smile. 'But yeah, I got it covered at least. There are a few of us on the team. Someone's always happy to step in.'

'Well...' He nods his head appreciatively. 'Don't you go stepping out on us now.' He pauses. 'I mean permanently, but breaks are fine.' He smiles. 'Luigi's, though... they do a mean carbonara.'

'Seriously, I'm fine.' I laugh. 'Go enjoy yourselves.' I'll have a rummage through the studio's kitchen after they've gone. There must be some biscuits still lying around from the auditions.

Terry shrugs. 'Our loss, but okay.' He's about to go when he stops in the doorway, turning back towards me, his features genuine. He's no longer joking. 'And thanks, Clara.'

'Thanks?'

'You saved the day.' He points one long, thin finger straight at me and gives me a wink. 'Star quality. Seriously. That's you.'

'Go.' I laugh, shooing him toward the door, eager to get back to work.

'Bye!' Terry and Jeff chorus, the door closing behind them with a bang.

Silence. I breathe out, the tension easing from my shoulders. Now I can finally focus without anyone distracting me. Cracking my knuckles, I dive back into the files, the familiar routine of organisation soothing my frazzled nerves. Terry appreciates me. He really does. This is where I belong – here, in this office, working behind the scenes to help launch new talent into stardom. Okay, so it's not the total dream fulfilled – I'm not launching myself, but that wouldn't be possible anyway. Who's ever heard of a solo singer with stage fright? It just doesn't stack up. In truth, I don't want to be out at some fancy Italian restaurant, pretending to enjoy small talk. I'm happy here, lost in the magic of making dreams come true.

The phone rings, shattering my concentration. I could leave

it, but that's maybe not the best thing to do. It could be anyone, maybe even Marco. I grab the receiver a little too quickly. 'Delagado Sounds, Clara speaking.' I get a thrill just saying the company name.

'Clara, it's Minty!' my brother's over-enthusiastic voice booms down the line.

'How did you get my–'

'Stan. I saw him down the pub. He told me what happened. Just watch out, babe, you know what those music people are like.'

My brother seriously dislikes this industry. My parents struggled to make a living for so long.

'It's fine.'

'Hmm,' he grunts. 'Besides, this is not exactly the best timing.'

'Sorry?'

'I've got a date lined up for you tonight. It's with a mate of mine.'

'Minty, no,' I groan. 'Why didn't you mention this yesterday!'

There's a beat of silence on the phone. 'Well… you were a bit down on my mates, to be honest.'

'With good reason.'

'Maybe but, look, this one I promise you, he's absolutely perfect.'

'I doubt it. What's the dress code? Anoraks, in time for the meal deal?'

'Not this one, sis. This guy is class. He's done university, the whole thing.'

'Minty!' I sigh.

'Just this once. If I get it wrong this time, seriously, never again.'

Now that is an offer almost too good to let slip. 'You mean that?'

'Yeah. Absolutely.'

I look at my crowded desk, it would be lovely to get Minty and his matchmaking off my back, but he couldn't have picked a worse moment. 'I can't do it tonight. It's been mad here. I'm exhausted.' I stare at the rows of unchecked digital files. 'And I haven't even finished yet.'

'Has to be tonight,' Minty returns, enthusiastically. 'He's only in town for one night. You can make time for him. Just this once?' There's the muffled sound of the phone being grabbed and passed over.

'Hi, Clara…'

It's Tim, my brother's best mate, his partner in crime. Tim had been on the scene the whole time I was growing up. He's kind of Minty's support network. Becoming a guardian must have been scary for my nineteen-year-old brother, but at least he had Tim there when he needed a buffer.

'His name's Robin,' Tim says eagerly. 'And Minty's right, lovely lad and great name. Don't you think that's a lovely name? Robin.'

I sink down in my chair. Why is my love life so public? 'Hi, Tim, the name is fine. It's just–'

'It's like Christmas,' Tim pipes up.

'Thanks for the clarity, but–'

The phone is passed again. Minty's back. 'I told him all about you, showed him photos.'

'Which photos?' Tim asks, his voice sounding slightly distant.

'The one at the water park.'

'In my bikini!' I shriek.

'Nah. The other one. When you're in the…'

'Kaftan thing,' Tim adds helpfully.

'Exactly,' Minty says. 'You're my sis, sis. No bikinis till you're married.'

'Minty.' My voice carries a warning note.

'Anyway,' my brother continues, 'Robin is super keen to meet my little sis!'

Oh dear. I massage my weary temples. The screen in front of

me blurs. I could do with a break, but not my brother's match-making. Although if this seriously was the last time…

'I'm not a child, Minty. I can find my own relationships.' There's now absolute silence from the other end of the line. 'I can!'

'Sure,' they both bluster together.

'Only,' Minty says, 'we know men.'

'Yeah.' Tim's voice booms. 'On account of the fact that we are…'

'Men.' Minty fills in Tim's missing words.

'So we're kind of on the inside loop,' says Minty.

'The inner circle, and we just want you to be happy.' Tim's voice sounds small, pathetic, but absolutely sincere.

'I can't,' I say, exhaling a long, low sigh. 'Even if I wanted to. I've got way too much work.'

'That new job?' Even Tim sounds excited.

'Oh, Tim, it's so good.' I glance around the office: at the gold records on the wall. At the guitars propped in corners. 'For once in my life, I feel like I'm in the exact right place.'

'Brilliant,' Minty says with genuine warmth.

'Couldn't happen to a nicer gal,' Tim adds.

I can hear Minty grunting in agreement. 'So, we just need to get that love life sorted. Only you'll need to come now.'

'Grrr.' I find myself gritting my teeth. 'I haven't finished logging this stuff.'

'Tomorrow,' Minty says.

'Get in early,' Tim adds.

'Sorted,' Minty drawls. 'Come on, Clara! You work too hard. You need to get out more. Robin's a great guy. You'll love him. Do this for me? Last time,' Minty wheedles, his voice taking on a pleading note.

'Last time?' I restate the offer, no one is wriggling out of it.

'The work will still be there tomorrow,' Tim says reasonably, 'but Robin won't. Come on, Clara. You need to have some fun!'

Despite everything, their words strike a chord. Maybe they have a point. I have seriously been working far too hard at this. I'm not even sure how they're going to pay me. Overworking is a part of who I am, but my life is a bit of a mess. I seriously need to start putting myself first. I stare at the spreadsheet in front of me. I could get in early and tie it up before everyone gets in. Wouldn't it be amazing if I could get all the elements of my life sorted: great job, wonderful man? I glance towards Marco's empty office. The man is gorgeous, but trouble, and my brother and Tim may have a point; maybe Robin really is worth a try? They've had so many duds that the odds are, at some point, they've got to come up trumps.

'I don't know,' I say slowly. 'I really don't think this is a good idea.' But even as I say the words, I know my resistance is crumbling.

Tim and Minty pounce.

'Come on, Clara! Live a little!'

'Do it for me,' Minty says sadly. 'I just want you to be happy!'

'It'll be fun,' Tim adds eagerly. 'We promise!'

I close my eyes. They always gang up on me like this to get their way. But Minty is my brother, and he cares about me, even if he has a clumsy way of showing it. Finally, I surrender.

'All right, all right. But if this is a disaster, I will never, ever, ever trust you with my love life again.'

A roar of triumphant laughter greets my words. 'Great, we're downstairs in the lobby.'

They're in the building!

'Get yourself down here quick.'

I cringe. I've told them so many times not to come into the lobby. They always leave something. The goblin mask is a case in point. 'Okay, but get yourselves back in the car. I'll come out.' They can do less damage that way. I hang up the phone and slump back in my chair with a groan. What have I gotten myself into?

When I emerge onto the street, Minty is waiting for me in an ancient hatchback, the engine rumbling. Tim and Minty cheer when they see me.

'You look gorgeous, C!' my brother says, eyes bright. 'Robin's going to be blown away!'

I roll my eyes as I slide into the back seat. I've been in this dress all day. I certainly don't feel gorgeous. 'I bet he's awful,' I say.

'Don't be daft,' Minty scoffs, his unruly hair flopping over his eyes as he pulls out into the road. The car vibrates in time with the radio. 'I have excellent taste in men.'

I clear my throat. 'Apart from the last three.'

'Sorry about that.' Minty winces. 'But Robin's going to be different.'

'We can feel it!' Tim adds enthusiastically.

I shake my head, stare at the streets sliding by the car. The city is glittering in the twilight.

Maybe, just maybe, my brother will get it right this time. Maybe this date won't be a total disaster after all. Maybe today is the day I nail everything: dream job, dream man, dream life. In the darkness of the back seat, I take a deep breath and smile.

Only, it is a disaster. The reason Robin is in town for one night only is because he lives with his mum. That kind of thing might tick my brother's boxes on the sensible and stable front, but the man is in his mid-thirties, and his mum does everything for him. She rang him three times whilst we were having a drink. It was a short date lasting precisely fifty-six minutes. I timed it. Not only does he live with his mum, he also works for her, and he managed to bore me rigid for over an hour, giving me details of his recent holiday – with his mum. He even showed me the accompanying snaps. It's true, he's good-looking enough. And okay, so he is kind of sweet, and his mum's done a great job of bringing him up and squeezing him into a two-piece, but there's no spark. Not even a fizzle. I have to admit, the shadow of work comes in mighty handy. It's a relief to be able to tell him that, actually, I've got a lot of urgent admin to do back at the office, and would he mind dropping me off at Delagado Towers? He didn't. Most likely, he wasn't getting any chemistry, either.

Once again, I cross the wide marble foyer, saying hi to the night porter before pressing the golden button for the lift. It's going to be a long night.

As I stand waiting, I pull out my phone and bring up the family group chat – Tim is also in it.

Strike.

I write.

You two are out.

That's the last time I go on a date set up by my brother or his mate. Next time, I'm going to find my own man.

CHAPTER 8

CLARA

The office suite is empty. The only light is coming from the glow of the computer screen in front of me. I blink hard, trying to focus on the rows of thumbnail images – the last batch of auditions that I have to log before I can head home.

I shouldn't have taken time out. I could have been home in bed by now. That's the last time I listen to my brother and his mate. My shoulders tense. I'm feeling so stressed. It's been a long and very odd day. The digits on the screen dance in front of my eyes. I take a moment to rub my forehead. Everything has to be perfect. Betsy will inspect my work with a magnifying glass, looking for any excuse to criticise. I might have only just met the woman today, but I know her type. If I give her an inch, she'll make my life a living hell, along with kicking me out of this job.

I stifle a yawn and double-check the titles, descriptions, and tags on the video files.

Soprano: 22. Good stage presence.
Contralto: 30. Nervous and arrogant. Difficult.

It's clear from the way Betsy wanted her notes taken that winning this competition is about a lot more than having a good voice. Then again, I guess they all had to have a good voice to get through the door.

At last, although my eyes are feeling scratchy and dry, I log the final entry for what has to be the biggest performance competition in the country. Within seconds, it has all been copied to the USB Betsy gave me. She seemed to have a thing about copying anything to the cloud or leaving info on the computers. Apparently, the company had been hacked a few years ago. That's why Betsy devised her own system, and heaven help anyone who steps out of line. It's been such a long day. I can't quite believe that only this morning, I had been sitting in reception, not a clue as to what was going on above my head, and now I'm here with the last file in order. I lean back in my chair and allow myself a deep intake of breath. It's all done. For just one moment, I let my thoughts wander. Closing my eyes, I imagine standing on the winner's stage, the spotlight shining down on me, bathing me in a warm glow. All the people I helped audition are there, and once again, they are giving me a standing ovation. Only this time, it's not for sorting out the admin; in my daydream, they're cheering me on because of my singing. Marco's there, looking incredible in a tuxedo, urging me to sing the last song of the evening. I tilt my head back, but nothing comes out. Not a squeak. Panic floods my model-made-up face. My jaw drops open way too wide. Everyone is waiting, waiting, waiting. But this isn't that kind of a game. Within a moment, the stage is swamped with other women, women in expensive, sparkling dresses and cost-a-fortune hairdos. Slack-jawed, I'm toppled from my stilettos and pushed to the back, out of sight, as they all open their mouths and sing perfectly.

At my desk, the daydream vanishes, and I sink my head down onto my arms. Is this all I'm good for, tidying up other people's mess? I scratch anxiously at the cuticle on one finger. Do I have to live my life in the background? How about if that clapping could be turned around? What if it wasn't simply my admin skills that were getting me attention. My voice is good and clear. As good as anything I'd heard today. I feel sure the panel would love me if I only got a chance to step out on that stage and managed to sing. Only that's never going to happen. Instead, if I'm lucky, I'll be destined to log auditions and pick up Marco's slack until the end of time, trapped in this dim little room that smells of stale pastries and broken dreams. My broken dreams.

'Stop,' I groan, grabbing my hair between both hands. I need to get home. This kind of self-sabotage is getting me nowhere. I did well today. That's what I need to hold on to. Tomorrow, I'm going to have to be Little Miss Organised all over again. I take the USB, an SD with the tracks on, and a slim one-sheet hard copy of the log that I've boiled any auditions of interest down to and place it all in Betsy's office, just as I've been instructed to do.

I grab Amy's bag, then check my phone to confirm that the bike I had booked to pick the item up is still okay to collect in the morning – thankfully it is. Resting my jacket over my shoulders, I switch off the lights, ready to head home for the night. But when I open the door to leave the office suite, I stop in my tracks. The door to the audition room is open. Just a crack, but enough to see the gleam of the electric baby grand and the mic standing ready and waiting. My heart thumps in my chest. Suddenly, I don't feel sleepy anymore.

The studio is empty and dark except for the moonlight filtering through the high windows. No one would know if I just sneaked in and recorded a track, because no one is here, which is exactly how I like it. I hesitate on the threshold, two emotions warring inside me: longing and fear. I know that this is daft. Reckless. I've just managed to get my foot on the stepladder to an environment I've always wanted to work in: the music industry. If Betsy found out I'd snuck into the recording studio, I'm willing to bet that I'd be fired on the spot.

Although… my brain starts to whir, they haven't actually hired me yet. When will I have another chance like this? That mic, standing in the middle of the room, so tall and slim, is calling to me like a siren's song. Damn, I take a deep breath and push the door open wider. The familiar scent of wood polish, mixed with the hangover odour of over-perfumed starlets, washes over me.

This is crazy. Then again, crazy and impulsive have got me this far. Why stop now?

Heart pounding, I step into the room. The door creaks softly behind me, swinging shut. I'm alone. The studio is mine.

I walk towards the mic as if in a dream, my heels clicking on the polished wood. Running my hands along the piano as I pass, feeling the cool ivory keys under my fingertips. This is my moment. I can sing anything I want. But I should probably be quick. I glance at my wristwatch. It's half twelve already. If I'm going to do this, I need to do it now.

I make my way to the control booth and flick on the lights, blinking in the sudden brightness. I'd watched Jeff earlier as he set everything up. I'm pretty sure I can remember which buttons to press. Under my fingers, the equipment comes to life with a satisfying buzz and a wink of lights as my heart races. I honestly could record something now. Give me an hour, and it would all be done. What harm could it do? A demo. Just one single track to show myself what I can do. No one has to know. I wouldn't even have to play it to anyone, but I would always have it – know that it could be done.

With trembling fingers, I reach forward and flick on the master switch. The recording equipment hums, ready and waiting. The next stop is the monitor. Within minutes it's on, bathing the room in a blue light. Quickly I scan through the tracks on the computer, searching for something that speaks to me. I just need a cover. Something I'm already familiar with. Jeff had set up a recording earlier in the day for a Donna Summer track. A soulful piano ballad with a driving beat and emotional lyrics about love, heartbreak, and finding your voice. Perfect.

Once I locate the track, I press play and step up to the mic as the music fills the booth. I close my eyes, letting the melody wash over me, feeling the rhythm in my bones. When the time is right, I open my mouth and sing. At first, my voice trembles, uneven and breathy. But with each note, it grows stronger, surer, until I'm pouring my heart into the music. Glancing up at the corner of the studio, I see the red light blinking above me, recording the riff. It doesn't get much better than this. I'm really doing it – singing professionally in a real studio. Even if no one ever hears this, as far as I'm concerned, I've made it.

CHAPTER 9

CLARA

The next morning, I click-clack my way through the swinging doors to the Tower, feeling a swell of excitement. Last night went well. I'm heading straight for the lifts. No more stopping at the reception desk.

'Hey, look at you,' Stan says, winking as I pass. 'Hear you saved the day yesterday.' He claps an appreciative burst of applause. 'That's my girl.'

'Thanks, Stan.' I stop to give him a hug.

He laughs.

'Was it okay, though?' I seriously don't want to put anyone out. 'Did you get cover for me?'

'Hmm.' He pulls back, giving me a hard look. 'Replace you? Not possible.' The stern face fades, and he cracks a smile. 'But yeah, the stand-in turned out okay.' He pats my shoulder. 'We managed. We will always manage. You set up the system so everything works. Glides along. So, now,' he leans in towards me conspiratorially, 'now you go on and fly, girl, just as high as those wings will take you. Everyone's rooting for you. All the kids who came down from that audition yesterday had nothing but praise.'

I grin from ear to ear. It's nice knowing you're appreciated.

It's worth almost as much as my pay cheque, which reminds me, I need to find out who's responsible for that now.

In the lift, I have to pinch my cheeks to stop myself from smiling. Wow, what a day yesterday was, but I survived. More than that, the project survived. No complaints. In fact, there's only been praise, and today, what I'm hoping for is a little more time to enjoy the full-on glamour of working in one of the leading recording studios in the capital. Without the tail end of the auditions, everything has surely got to be fifty per cent calmer. I take a sigh of relief and pat down my golden curls as I turn to face the sliding door. Curls that have been tonged to a 250-degree inch of perfection this morning. With my smile coming into line just as the golden doors pull back, only then do I realise I'm not going to get my wish for peace.

The office is a war zone: papers strewn everywhere, desks overturned, coffee mugs shattered on the floor. My blood freezes in my veins as I scan the chaos. What the hell is going on?

Marco storms past. 'Thank Christ for that. You can help us search,' he says, pulling the seat cushions off all the sofas.

'Well, they won't be there.' Betsy is standing in the doorway to her office, a scowl already on her face and it's not even nine o'clock.

'W-what?' I stutter.

'The auditions,' Marco growls, pushing Betsy out of the way. 'They're missing. The ones you were logging last night.'

Betsy gives me a hard look. 'It's all your fault.'

Oh no. My heart is fluttering in panic mode. I'm dead. Marco is going to kill me. Just as that thought skitters through my head, I'm forced to duck under the nearest desk to avoid a projectile flying fast across the room. A stapler, by the looks of it. Marco's rage certainly does manifest itself in many forms.

'Who left the blasted door open last night?' his voice thunders through the room.

'Doesn't matter.' Betsy shakes her head. 'When that woman,'

she points to me, still cowering under the desk, 'finished logging stuff. She should have put it on the USB, in my in-tray, out of sight. Like I showed her.'

Cowering under the desk, my face burns as I scan quickly back through my mind. It had been late. I grabbed my coat. I'd stopped off in the studio. I was so sure I'd dropped everything in Betsy's office when I'd finished. But that didn't matter, because I couldn't remember if I had closed the door to the studio when I left. Hot tears prick the back of my eyes. I just can't remember. I'm so tired, I seriously can't remember.

Marco storms over, grabbing me by the ankle.

'Don't yank her,' Betsy says. 'If you yank her, HR will get involved, and then it'll all turn into some poor-me intern saga.'

'I wasn't going to yank her.' His voice sounds mad as hell. He pushes my ankle gently to one side so my body twists around to face him, throwing one hand towards me to help me out. 'I can't interrogate her if she's under the bloody table, can I? What would HR think about that?' Gently, he pushes his arm towards me again.

I seriously don't care what HR will think about it. This is terrifying.

Betsy throws her arms up in the air and raises her eyes in a 'don't shoot me' gesture as though washing her hands of the interaction in case it gets nasty while I take the hand Marco's offering. My first thought, which is so not what my first thought should be, is wow, he has such soft skin. Maybe it's because I'm terrified. Maybe it's because I haven't had enough sleep, but either way his touch feels… gorgeous. My brother's always tinkering with cars. His friends are always tinkering with cars. I didn't know men could have hands that soft. And as I'm eulogising about this man's hands, I feel my brain throwing self-doubt and irritation into the mix; I cannot believe I've blown everything, this job, everything.

As I crawl ungracefully to my feet, I wince, bracing myself for the impact of his words. Yet, his tone is softer than Betsy's. Gentler. Less judgemental. 'Did you see anything, Clara?'

I stare up at him, wide-eyed and trembling. How can I admit it was me? I had doubled back to the office, worked late, used all of his million-dollar equipment to record myself singing, and then left the door open so a crack team of cat burglars could lift everything! He'll sack me on the spot. I need this job. It was supposed to be my first step on the music production ladder. Besides, he also has the power to sack me from my reception job. I have rent to pay and a brother to clear up after, and...

'Clara!' Marco gives my hand a light shake.

Why are we still holding hands? I'm not sure.

'The recordings...' he says softly. 'Did you see anything?'

'I-I'm sorry, Mr Delagado,' I stammer. 'I didn't see anything. I got here just now, same as you.'

The lie slips out before I can stop it. But I refuse to correct myself. I'm simply not brave enough. I have no intention of telling him about my late-night visit. My heart hammers so loud against my ribs I swear it'll give me away. Marco searches my face and for one long, hard moment, I'm convinced he is absolutely going to see through me. What is it that liars do? Avoid eye contact? I think so. I think that's it. I stare straight back at him, unflinching, feeling my body cave with relief as he releases me with a snort.

'Useless,' he mutters, kicking a chair aside. 'All of you, useless!'

I breathe a quiet sigh of thankfulness. If there is a God, believe me, I am praying. Even though my hands are shaking and I'm feeling wrecked by my panicked surge of adrenalin. I've bought myself a little more time to fudge myself out of this situation, but if I don't find those audition tapes, I know I'm done for.

MARCO

An hour later and we're still all huffing and puffing around the office. 'This is unbelievable,' I vent. 'All that work, all that hassle, all those people.'

Betsy raises one eyebrow. 'All that smiling?'

'I managed to prop up my smile just fine,' I say, emptying the drawers in reception, all of them.

'It's that girl,' Betsy mutters under her breath. There's no need for the thinly veiled passive-aggressive attitude, though a lower tone might have been handy – Clara is in the studio, looking under all the equipment.

Betsy glances in Clara's direction. 'The other one was fine.'

I don't need to look at Betsy to know she's scowling. Nothing and no one will ever be good enough for Betsy.

'I leave you for five minutes,' she barks.

She's doing her usual and getting right under my skin. I decide to toss the blame back. 'Why do you have to have such a complicated way of storing stuff? Who even uses USBs anymore?'

Betsy shoots me a withering look. 'I've had stuff crash on me many times. Even the cloud's not totally reliable. Not after the last incident they had here. Call me old-fashioned, but a hard drive is safer.'

I can't say anything to that. Nothing. It is so clearly not *safer.* 'So, what do we do, start from scratch? Weeks of work, wasted. Because it's not just the audition, it's calling the buggers in, setting times. Stroking egos.' I feel like I'm going to throw up. I'm not good with people. The audition season is about as bad as it gets for me. 'Not to mention getting the musicians on call!'

I kick an empty coffee cup, deliberately, sending it skittering across the floor, dregs of coffee slopping out onto the carpet in a curiously irritating pattern. Sod's law, just my luck, Clara chooses that very moment to come back into the reception area. I must look like a grade-A arrogant idiot. She flinches. I don't blame her. The poor woman has already narrowly missed a stapler this morning. No way is she going to want to be hosed down with cold coffee. I have to get a grip. But every inch of my body is taut as a wire about to snap. Any other year, this kind of admin mess-up wouldn't have mattered. It would have been a pain, but I would have been able to work my way out of it. When Dad dropped out of the picture, I just had to please myself. But this year, I have shareholders watching my every move. Shareholders in the dragon lady forms of Betsy and Fitz. Fitz, I can handle. Probably. Only sometimes, I can't help but get the feeling that everyone would dearly love for me to fail. Isn't that the story people can't get enough of? Inherited everything and blew it away in next to no time. Don't people love that old chestnut?

One by one, the others are filtering into the studio. Terry and Jeff are exchanging wary looks. They've been on the wrong side of my temper before, but I refuse to pull back; this situation is a mess.

'Did any of you see the SDs last night?' I practically bite their heads off.

Terry shrugs. 'Hey, not my department.'

Jeff shoots the new girl a look. Sometimes, Jeff is such a sneak.

'And?' I say, giving him my mean eyes, the ones I perfected at boarding school. The ones that say, don't mess with me. Spit any accusations you have out on the table. If words could kill, Jeff would be a pile of ashes now. He shrugs.

'I logged everyone in,' Clara says, so quietly I can barely hear her. 'If we need to re-audition. I've got all their names on the front desk. Well, most of them. And maybe, if you can remember who you thought was good that would help. Even if you can't remember names, what they were singing, wearing, I could possibly trace them through that.'

I sink back onto the leather couch. Feeling thankful as hell that at least someone has some kind of solution. But I'm not one to show any sign of gratefulness. Gratefulness is for the weak, that was one of my dad's mantras. There's no need to be grateful when you pay people. My dad may have been the worst person in the world, but somehow, those mantras of his, they just kind of stuck. 'Go on then,' I grunt, pulling my phone from my pocket. 'Get busy.'

CLARA

Marco leans back in a leather swing chair so large it looks like it belongs to some kind of Masters of the Universe cartoon character. His muscled arms are clasped casually behind his head as he tells us all to get busy. I'm not totally convinced that anything he's saying right now is helpful, but it seems like when Marco says jump, we all have to do just that.

'What the f-ing hell.' A new voice cuts into my thoughts.

I turn to see the most gorgeous young woman standing in the doorway, tall and skinny with shiny black hair so glossy you can practically see your face in it. It hangs in a shimmering curtain right the way down to her hips. I can almost hear it swish as she walks. She looks like some kind of human-sized doll. Can skin seriously be that flawless without photo editing? Only, the odd thing is, out of the corner of my eye, I'm not sure if I'm imagining it, but Marco seems to bristle. I mean, he was bristling before, but with the entrance of this uber-goddess, the man is practically growing porcupine spines.

'Fitz,' he says gruffly. 'You shouldn't be here.'

He jumps up from the chair, leaving it swinging in his wake, and slips an arm around the woman's skinny, bare shoulders. She's wearing practically nothing. Then again, if I had her body, I'd be doing the same. Are they an item? It feels like they kind of are. They look amazing together. Two peas out of the same classy pod. She's sporting this gorgeous crochet crop top vest and a suede mustard skirt. Both items have barely more width than a belt. I suppose the boots are doing a lot of coverage. They're thigh high, suede, laced, and with platforms so thick, this woman is almost skimming the clouds.

'Hey.' She shakes his arm loose and strides into the room. 'New girl?' she says, peering at me over the top of her pink-tinted glasses.

'Clara,' I say, because I feel I need to say something, just to prove that I do actually speak.

'Oh wow.' She rolls her eyes. 'He sure gets through them.'

Betsy pulls her large lips into a pout. 'Well, this one here might just be the quickest exit in the planet's history. She's lost everything. The whole damn show.' Betsy scowls.

I squirm.

'Hey,' Terry says, coming to my rescue. 'Actually, that's not strictly true. Someone broke into the studio late last night. The place was burgled. The logs, the recordings, it's all missing.'

I like Terry's story so much better.

'Oh dear,' Fitz says on an exhale that's practically a yawn. 'Bang goes the big promo breakfast bash tomorrow. Shame, my dress was wowzer.'

She could wear an Elastoplast and it would look wowzer.

She tilts her head to one side. 'Cancelling, that's going to look *sooo* bad.'

I can see why Marco doesn't want her here. She has an awkward habit of stating the obvious with the subtlety of a wrecking ball.

'It might not be a total wipeout,' Marco says, taking in a deep breath.

Curiously, I notice that this goddess woman is as slippery as an eel every time he walks towards her. She simply seems to evaporate away.

'We can bluff through the breakfast, Betsy.' Marco shoots a look towards her. 'Call the press, make some kind of excuse.'

Betsy puts her hands on her wide, gate-like hips. 'Do I get a please with that?'

'I can give a noncommittal press statement,' I say. What with all the bickering and blame bouncing around, this is going nowhere. Someone needs to take control of the situation. They all stare at me like I've just teleported down from Mars.

There's an awkward pause in which everyone seems to be wondering what the next step should be.

Then Fitz shoots me a wide smile. 'Fab, this young woman can do the press thing. Because you,' she snakes her arms around Marco's neck, 'are taking me out for breakfast.'

My heart sinks. So, I was wrong about the avoiding thing, they're clearly keen to get their hands on each other. Maybe they're just not keen on company? Of course, he's in a relationship and, of course, she's gorgeous. With his looks, she has to be. Only...

'Now?' Marco's forehead criss-crosses into a thousand worry lines. 'But I have to–'

'Shareholders meeting,' Fitz says lightly, but there's an authoritative air of finality about her tone. She shrugs. 'Let the others sort out the mess. I'm a shareholder. I demand attention.'

I've never seen anyone look so irritated. Marco's face is colouring an odd shade of puce. His arms flapping around his body like a drowning man tangled up with a man-eating octopus. Most likely, he's keen to sift through what we have left of those recordings and nail down some recalls.

'It'll wait,' Fitz says languidly. 'But my stomach won't. I need pancakes.'

How on earth she manages to keep that figure and eat pancakes mystifies me more than the fate of the audition tapes.

Betsy's eyes narrow as she fixes Marco under her gaze. 'I just want it sorted. End of,' she says before storming out, not offering up her breakfast plans.

'Has anyone checked the CCTV footage?' I ask, hoping against hope that the floor doesn't have any kind of surveillance. Everyone turns and looks at me blankly. Perhaps I'm in luck. I take a beat. Maybe they didn't understand because, surely, looking at the CCTV footage would be the first thing anyone in their right mind would do?

'On it,' Marco says, pulling one hand through his dark curls. 'Yup.' He nods. 'I've asked security.'

This could be very bad for me. It was okay working late, they all knew I had done that, but I had returned to the office after hours. I'd switched on all the lights, tied up the work, then opened the studio and ran myself a session. How was I going to explain that? But things are already moving forward. I have to keep up; any minute now, they're going to find out about my midnight singing, and I need to be ready.

'Does anyone know exactly what's missing?' Jeff says, glancing around the studio, puzzled.

Marco sighs. 'Mainly stuff from Betsy's office. That's where all the finalised audition tapes were. All on one SD card. And there were a couple of Heritage guitars. None of the mixing equipment. There are other bits and pieces of recordings, but nothing's organised. You'd have to listen to two weeks of duds to make any sense of it.' He flicks a case on the desk. 'Not logged, but…'

'I can do all that,' I offer. 'I can listen and log. I can probably remember some of the comments.'

'Well,' Jeff says, 'that's a plus. I thought the girl with the tattoos yesterday was good. Liked her style. She was singing a Madonna song.'

Marco pushes a tape idly into the deck.

'And I'm pretty sure there was a girl on Monday,' Terry pipes up. 'Hmm.' He looks thoughtful. 'Could have been Wednesday? Taylor Swift number.'

Both men shake their heads. From my stint of logging the auditions, I remember there were a lot of Taylor Swift numbers. That's not going to help narrow things down.

It's going to be difficult to piece together every person that auditioned. This is a nightmare. I feel myself flush guiltily. It's all my fault. I was the last one in here. I must have left the door open. Luckily, no one has any idea about this. No one will know until they watch the CCTV footage. At the thought of them watching the footage, my body breaks out into a hot flush. My whole being flares as hot as an Olympic torch. It's at this exact moment that Marco glances over at me. Attention is the last thing I need. I turn my back on him and pretend to be looking at a clipboard.

'Are you okay?' he asks, and it genuinely sounds as if he's concerned.

'Yes,' I say with a brightness I am clearly not feeling. 'It's just… I should get on with this.'

'Well,' Fitz says, with an equal brightness, only hers seems genuine. Not surprising since Fitz didn't bugger up two weeks' worth of auditions, so I guess she can afford the jaunty tone. 'Looks like you've all got your little old plans sorted, so…' She snakes an arm around Marco's waist.

Suddenly, my heart sinks and this time it's not the proximity of this glorious goddess to a man I would so love to attach myself to. No, this time, the sinking heart has a much more tangible target; a familiar melody blasts through the speakers, a Donna Summer track, and a shiver runs down my spine. I know that song. I recorded a version of it just yesterday. The intro plays out slowly. It's probably not my recording, I think. There's no need to panic. I'd used someone else's soundtrack. But horror of horror, my knees falter as my voice echoes out from the speakers, soft and clear, right on note, every decibel mine. I would love for the floor to just swallow me right then and there without a trace. But, since there's no earthquake on the horizon, I lunge towards the sound deck, desperate to remove the thing.

'I think that's a...' I feel the colour rising in my cheeks. My face is so hot it's practically sizzling. My fingers reach out, inches from the stop button.

'Hey.' Marco grabs my hand. His eyes widen, and for one earth-stopping moment, his deep brown eyes gaze into mine.

Irritated, Fitz rocks forward onto the balls of her toes. 'Marco?' she whines.

'Shh,' he says sharply.

Hands out defensively, as if warding me off, he lets the track play on, staring at the speakers in something like wonder. I freeze in place, panic, and a curious sense of exhilaration wars inside me. Actually, I sound okay.

When the whole thing has played through, there's absolute silence in the office. Silence until Marco raps one hand in a sharp trill across the reception counter. 'Did you all hear that? Did you hear that amazing voice?' His eyes are shining in ecstasy.

I swallow hard, struggling to keep my expression neutral. 'I... it was lovely, yes,' I say in my smallest voice ever, in case they recognise it from the track that's just been blaring on all speakers through the studio. 'Very talented.'

'Wow,' Jeff says.

Terry smiles. 'That there, that's our winner.'

'Was that just...' Betsy appears in her doorway. 'Who was that?'

'I liked it,' Fitz says with a shrug. 'Definitely, I'd say we go with that one. She was lovely.'

'Lovely?' Marco scoffs. 'That was transcendent. Angelic. Perfection given form.'

Fitz rolls her eyes once again as if to say he's always so over the top.

'Well?' Marco barks.

Everyone looks blank.

'Come on, who is she? What day was she in? A voice like that, someone must remember.'

Everyone looks blank.

Betsy crosses her arms over her large chest. 'If I had heard a voice like that, I would have remembered.'

I'm saying nothing. There are two practically priceless guitars missing from the walls and a whole mess of an admin situation going on because I happened to leave the door to the studio open. No way am I going to tell them it's my voice on the tape, and there's not a chance in hell that I'm going to admit to recording it late last night just before the office got turned over.

Marco drags a hand down his face with a groan. 'Christ, I'm losing my mind. That voice. Clara…' He turns to me.

Yet again, I feel weak at the knees; what the hell am I going to do now? He's found me out. Those guitars are worth more than my mortgage. I'm brewing a crush on an unachievable love interest. He's…

'You said you signed everyone in downstairs?'

I nod, relief washing over me. 'Maybe I missed a few, but most of them I got because of the lanyards. I can tie that in with the call sheets.' Useful, I think to myself, just hold on to being useful.

'Great.' He draws in a long breath.

'But…' Jeff is frowning. 'I just don't remember that…' He waves towards the deck. 'I mean, I'm pretty sure I would if I'd heard it.'

Terry scratches his chin. 'Maybe we didn't see her. Is there anything else on that tape?'

Jeff rewinds it through the machine. 'No, it's blank apart from that one song.'

'Hmm.' Terry's eyes narrow. 'It's kind of odd, don't you think?'

'I mean, we would definitely have noticed a voice like that.' Jeff stares at the tape.

'So,' Marco says, drawing out the word. 'You're thinking

maybe someone brought a demo tape in and just left it? They didn't audition, so we didn't hear them live?'

I have no intention of getting involved in this. 'Anyone want breakfast?' I ask brightly. I'd love to be anywhere but here.

'No,' all the men say together, as though they've got good old Evelyn waving her conductor's baton to keep them in sync.

'Next, you're going to say it was the burglar!' Betsy laughs unkindly, but I can't help noticing that she hasn't crossed her arms. She's intrigued by the voice, too.

Marco takes the cassette in his fingers. 'These are pretty standard. Get them anywhere.'

Like in this very studio, I think, but I'm clearly not going to add that kind of *useful* to the mix.

'My guess is,' Marco nods his head sagely, 'someone left it here by accident. One of the auditions. Someone came in to support a friend auditioning and...'

'So.' Jeff smiles, the bright spark of an idea catching in his eyes. 'They might not even have been auditioning. It could even be a professional, a teacher, or someone they're trying to emulate.'

Marco nods. 'Wouldn't you?'

'Marco,' Fitz whines. 'You've found your "voice". Let's go for brekky. The guys can handle it from here.' She glances around the room. 'Right, boys?'

I don't know how I fit in with the 'boys' but I get the feeling I'm included.

'If you want to find this woman,' Fitz continues. 'I mean, yes, she was good. I like the tune thing. Although it was kind of old, so I'm guessing she's old.'

Donna Summer is a classic, but I don't bother to pick her up on that.

'People will know her. Just go to all the clubs in town.' Fitz shrugs easily. 'If she's that good, she's bound to be singing somewhere.'

'Ah ha!' Marco jumps up from where he's been perched and spins Fitz around in a whirl like she is just the brightest and the best. Like they're kids. Just like they're kids.

In turn, Fitz tips back her head and laughs. 'You are crazy, Marco Delagado.'

Oh dear, I think, watching with envy as she does a full rotation, her dark curtain of hair spinning, her white teeth flashing like a lighthouse, his lovely thick, tanned arms wrapped around her tiny waist. This man is clearly not available.

'And you, Fitz, have the best ideas,' Marco says as he pulls away from her.

I feel sick. He's clearly in love with this woman. Of course, he is. Who wouldn't be?

'Clara, get on with redoing the call sheets, just in case,' he throws out.

Well, that's me sorted, I think, feeling my shoulders cave at the thought – Mrs Dogsbody.

Betsy frowns. 'Aren't you forgetting something?'

Marco scowls.

'Clara isn't even on the payroll.'

Marco shoots Betsy a hard look. 'Then get her a contract. We've got work to do.'

Fitz laughs. 'I love it when you act all big and bossy, Marco Delagado. I'll just…' She waves her arm behind her. 'Little girl's room.'

Seriously? *Little girl's room?* It's like someone abandoned a toddler at a theme park. I eye Marco cautiously. Perhaps that's it, they're both like children when they're together. Is this how all rich people act? Maybe it's because they simply don't have to come face to face with reality. Okay, so it was me that caused the panic, but for some reason, Fitz has no true grasp as to what kind of a problem she's just minced out of. The woman is supposed to be a shareholder! She may be beautiful, but she does seem a little vacant. We may have located a voice, a voice that is, of course, totally unsuitable because it's mine. But all this is beside the point. Does Fitz have any idea as to the severity of the situation? She may be gorgeous to look at, but what's a man like Marco doing with that... that... I so want to call her an airhead. I really do, but somehow, there's something so childishly joyous about her that I can't help thinking it would be wonderful to be Fitz. Even for an hour. Just to be that carefree. Just to have a man like Marco on my arm and a glowing life ahead of me, one in which it doesn't matter if any given situation goes belly-up, there's always pancakes for breakfast in a perfect world.

People like Fitz skate through life. It will never be her dealing the bad news; standing in front of the media-hungry press gangs, telling them we've lost the auditions and have no idea who should have won. It wouldn't even occur to her to get worried. It was somebody else's problem.

'And, Clara,' Marco says, rewinding the tape. Playing it, letting my recorded voice spill out once again into the room. 'You're with me tonight, scouring the clubs.'

There's no, do you mind? Or, are you busy; or, sorry to trouble you with this, but could you? Nope. Marco is a man who just expects star jumps if called for. Normally, that would get so far up my nose I'd probably be incapable of breathing, so why in the hell am I standing there all bright-eyed and simpering, nodding my head as though I'm two bacon and egg sandwiches short of the full, cognitive Monty?

CHAPTER 10

CLARA

'But you can't go back out,' Minty shouts at me as I push past him on my way up the stairs. 'You've only just got in.'

Sometimes, my brother is the master of the understatement.

I stop and give him a hard stare. He's standing at the bottom of our narrow staircase, his hands filthy from changing oil on some jalopy. The sooner this planet gets itself eco, the sooner our bathroom won't end up looking like a grease monkey's paradise every night.

'You do a quick turnaround on the night out front all the time,' I say.

In reality, he never stops working. His nights out are normally with Tim in front of the TV with a beer, which is not a night out. His idea of a great date is for a girl's car to break down. Not so that he can take advantage, no, so that he can get his head under the bonnet and get the thing fixed.

'That's different,' he says, massaging his fingers with a rag so dirty it doesn't belong in a domestic dwelling. 'You work too hard, Clara. You're always stuck behind a desk.'

'No.' I take a moment to pause on the stairs and turn towards him. 'This new job is different. Flexible hours, a lot more independence and responsibility.'

'They given you a contract?'

I clear my throat awkwardly. 'Not yet but...'

'It's not a job then. No contract, no job.'

Minty is always being done over by people wanting a quick fix, so he's wary of anyone standing in part-time. I know my unpaid, uncontracted promotion is going to be a tricky thing for him to digest. He's happy with me in an office – secretarial work, reception – and being paid for the hours that I clock in, but he has a problem with jobs that promise big titles but end up spiralling into unpaid overtime and promises that never come to fruition. So, I'm keen to avoid discussion. I don't need Minty to tell me that my move to the seventeenth floor could be temporary. If Marco and Co find out it was me that left the door open, I'm toast. Betsy will take joyous told-you-so delight in giving me the boot. Once that CCTV footage comes in, being helpful isn't going to stop my speedy decline. But maybe that's all beside the point. Maybe I just need to live for the moment. I'm about to go out to some fancy club with the most gorgeous man I've met in ages. Strike that – the most gorgeous man I've met in my life. Okay, so he's bad-tempered, moody, arrogant, a little too fond of the bottle, and is in the habit of throwing stationery. However, putting all of that to one side, Marco is the first man who's had my heart racing in forever.

'You would not believe the day I've had.' Minty leans on the banister below me. He always says this. I truly believe that I know exactly what kind of day he's had. It'll involve boiler suits, an inability to get a part, and a long tirade about the price of rubber. Unfortunately, tonight, he's in no need of an interested 'Oh?' from me. He's already dashing forward with the next subject in hand. The topic he is refusing to let drop – me and my evening plans.

'So, who are you going out with?' He sniffs, and I get the

distinct feeling that if Minty isn't satisfied with the answer, he might, despite the fact I'm in my twenties, attempt to ground me.

'The boss,' I say, trying to keep my tone as casual as possible when my heart is racing faster than a drummer in a rock band finale.

'A man?' His eyes narrow.

'Sure, why not?' I shrug. 'It's just work related.' I turn and head up towards my room. I don't have long to get myself glammed up.

'What about Robin?' My brother calls after me.

'Minty!' I stare down at him from the landing. 'I told you. Tonight is business.' This is kind of true. 'Besides, Robin's not my type.' This is absolutely true.

My brother looks confused, bordering on dumbfounded, as he follows me up the stairs. 'He's a nice lad. His mum speaks highly of him.'

That just about says it all, but apparently not because Minty is now in my bedroom. I raise one eyebrow. 'Bro, I don't have time for this. I have a work do. I could be on for a promotion.'

He shakes his head solemnly. 'But they need to give you a contract.'

'In hand,' I say, keeping my tone short. 'They were talking about it just a few hours ago, you know how these things take time. And if I do get a pay rise, I promise there'll be strawberries in the fridge every week.'

His smile runs from ear to ear. Minty is a man of childish pleasures and moral codes that can be bought off with a multitude of cheap treats. He's a true love. Give him a punnet of fresh fruit, and he'll be yours for life.

'So.' I widen my eyes and swish my hands towards him in an attempt to usher him out of my room. 'I need space.'

But curiously, Minty's not moving. 'What's he like? This boss. How old?'

'In or out?' I say firmly. 'And if you're staying, I warn you, I'm going to be swanning around in undies and lacquering on the hairspray.'

'Ew.' He backs out.

I don't need any more of an invitation. I shut the door on him.

'And you'll be back early?' his muffled voice asks through the closed door.

'Absolutely.' I loosen the belt on my office dress and go straight for my wardrobe. 'I've got work in the morning, and I've been at it all day. This is not a late one.'

'Okay,' Minty says. He doesn't sound happy, but he doesn't sound like he's going to treat me to the 'none shall pass' routine on the stairs.

I throw back my wardrobe door. My clothes are packed in way too tightly, there's so much stuff you can barely see what you're looking for. Suddenly, I don't feel quite so full of myself anymore. Sure, I've got lots to wear, but not one thing suitable for a night on the town with Marco Delagado. The only expensive, decent clothes I've got are the things I wear to work. Then again, he hasn't seen me in those because he has his own lift and doesn't come through reception, not unless I happen to be wearing a goblin mask! Okay, I think to myself, sinking down on the bed and running my eyes across the evening's possibilities. I improvise. I can wear one of my work dresses. I have a smart shirt dress with gold buttons and a neat collar that I bought last year in a sale. It's only had a couple of outings behind the reception desk. It might not be high fashion, but it's the most expensive, least worn-looking thing that I've got. I'll just jump in the shower, do my hair, and all will be fine.

I grab my luxury washbag with my night out treats and head to the bathroom. The sink is filthy.

'Minty! How many times... Do not wash off in here after work,' I shout.

'What?' Minty grunts from somewhere downstairs.

'Use the garage for washing your hands. Don't...' Oh, what

does it matter? He's so un-house trained. He's over thirty. There's no hope. I switch on the tap. It's cold. Icy cold.

'MINTY!'

I hear him thundering up the stairs.

'There's no water.' I could practically cry. I'm exhausted. It's been a long, hard, and confusing day, and this is the last thing I need.

'There's no water,' I repeat, but this time with a sob.

He glances guiltily at the shower, at the black sink, at the rags he's left on the floor. It's a mess, and the blame lies totally at his door.

Sheepishly, he hides his hands behind his back, dropping his head in a don't-notice-me attitude. 'I'll, ugh, I'll put the immersion on.'

I feel myself biting the insides of my mouth to try and avoid blasting him out of the universe. 'Yup. You do that.'

That is when the light in the bathroom goes dead.

My dear sweet and infuriating brother glances nervously up at the fitting. 'Could be the bulb.'

But the hallway is dark, too. 'Minty, did you pay the electric bill?'

'Um.' He chews his bottom lip. 'I meant to. I just.'

'Grrr… Out. Out. Out!' I push him back through the door, slamming it in his wake.

MARCO

She's standing there in front of me – Clara. The girl we hired today. The one with the blonde hair and all the curves. She went home to get changed. That's what she said. She told me she was going to get dressed up.

'No,' I say simply. We're supposed to be going to RJ King's, one of the best jazz clubs in town; if the voice on the tape is singing anywhere in the city, that's where she has to be. I've got the tape. King must know the girl. He's like a walking encyclopaedia on talent. The music industry is just worlds within worlds. Everyone knows everyone. But this isn't going to work because she, the girl, this Clara, is wearing... Hmm, I'm not even sure what you'd call it. Office wear. Librarian wear. Euthanasia-appropriate attire. And then there's the hair. What in the hell happened to the hair?

'What...' She glances down at herself.

The way she does it, the uncertainty, it is actually quite endearing. Fitz would give me a black eye if I tried to interfere with her fashion choices. Then again, Fitz knows what to wear and when.

I steeple my hands in front of my face. Clearly, I'm going to have to spell out the problem. 'We're going to a nightclub, an expensive nightclub. You can't look like you've just come straight from work.' It's some kind of shirt thing, slightly fitted, which is nice, but it's a dull-as-ditch-water grey and the obscene eighties-style gold buttons shot down it like a military general make her look as stiff and uninteresting as said military general.

She blushes, and I guess I've hit the nail on the head. This is exactly what she wears to work. The blue outfit she'd been sporting earlier was just a lucky dip out of the closet.

She furrows her brow, puts one small hand up to her face, like kids do when they're about to blush, or sob. She doesn't even pretend to be okay with the criticism. This woman is so transparent, so honest. Being with her, I feel kind of raw. Kind of naked. Bugger. I walk to the other side of the table. Sit down and try to look irritated rather than curious. She's in the worst fashion choice I've seen in years, so why do I find her so magnetic? Despite the outfit, I'm reluctant to take my eyes from her.

'I'll call a taxi,' I say, reaching for the phone.

Her pretty face shifts to one side, in an attitude of curiosity. 'I thought we were going to walk?' She sounds confused.

The club isn't far. We were going to walk, but that plan's dead in the water now. Odd, because I was actually looking forward to the walk. A stroll through the streets. They're lit with lamps this time of year and giving off that sulphurous glow that reminds you of early autumn. I could have maybe slipped my arm around her if she got cold, I could… I give myself a shake. This is seriously not the time or the person to be striking up a relationship with. That was my dad all over. He split up with my mum after she found him in this very office, naked, over the mixing desk with the secretary, the receptionist, and the saxophone player. Maybe I am lucky. Maybe I inherited the man's business, but there's no way I'd want to inherit his personality.

CLARA

I knew there was something wrong as soon as he looked at me. I'd been worrying about being too dressy, but it seemed as though I had pushed my look way too far back the other way. I'm getting this excruciatingly awkward feeling that Marco's embarrassed to be seen walking down the street with me. He called a taxi straight off, and the club isn't far from the Towers. In fact, it will take longer by cab, seeing as the offices are wrapped in a massive one-way system. I'm kind of beginning to wish I'd never taken a single step away from that reception desk in the foyer. This is not my world. I don't have the right clothes for it, the right words for it, and I've already seriously messed up all Marco's work. I'm beginning to wish I'd stayed home with Minty.

It's then that Marco slides open a drawer and pulls out a bundle of papers.

'Contract,' he says, brusquely. 'You should sign it tonight, so we can get you on the system.'

I stare at the neat booklet in front of me, with its embossed logo. Isn't this exactly what I wanted? But I hesitate.

Once they find out I was the one who left the door open, I'll be out on my ear. Can they threaten legal action against me? Is it incompetence? Of course it is. Am I better being contracted or saying I was just a stand-in, just helping? I am so screwed. But working in the music industry is a dream come true. I pick up the pen and flick through the pages, it's all standard stuff, with enough of a pay raise for strawberries for my brother and few new additions to my wardrobe. I want this job. I sign. Marco witnesses. I'm just going to have to take one day at a time, but one thing is for absolute certain – I've got to do something about that CCTV footage.

I had left a message on Stan's answerphone asking if he could stall handing it over. Stan might not work in security, but he knows everyone in the building, and they all seem to owe him a favour. Maybe I could just edit my bit out and then give them the rest of the footage, the part where the criminals burst through the door and nick the guitars. Guitars and admin. Because that is, after all, the only element the police will be interested in. Although something's not stacking up. For the life of me, I can't work out why anyone would steal Betsy's admin. Then again, I'm not one hundred per cent sure Stan will be able to help. So, I know I didn't commit a crime, but the guitars are worth a fortune. This has to be a police matter. If it's in their hands already, there'll be no stopping this snowball.

All this is bubbling around in my head as we exit the building. The cold air of the street hits me as we step out of Marco's private lift and jump into a taxi. Despite the worry, I still can't quite believe my luck. Okay, so this might be business but I happen to be out on the town with the most glorious man.

Live for the moment, I remind myself, taking a deep breath as the streets outside the taxi blur into an eclectic pattern of light and dark. I did nothing wrong. I didn't actually steal anything. It was just a…

'Clara.' Marco's voice jolts me back to the present. 'We're here.'

Confused, I glance out of the door. We are so not here. I may never have set one foot inside the door of RJ King's, but I sure as hell know it's not down some dark alley. I peer anxiously out of the cab window.

'Well, get out,' Marco says, opening his own door and getting out.

I glance nervously at the driver. He offers a search-me shrug.

Hmm, none of this is making sense. But Marco's already turning, walking away down the backstreet, his shoes echoing against the high walls of industrial buildings.

'Hurry up,' he shouts without turning. 'We don't have all night.'

My heart sinks. It's drugs. He's clearly got some kind of habit. I don't do drugs. My parents had dabbled and it never did them any good. I'm trying to build a life I want to be in, not escape from.

'Clara!' He turns to me, his deep voice bellowing down the corridor of silent blank walls.

'Coming,' I say with all the brightness of a lapdog. Sometimes I irritate myself so much. This is not all right. I don't want to be in contact with any tail end of the drug trade. It doesn't matter if it's just for personal use. I don't want to get involved, and yet here I am, hurrying grudgingly along behind a man I barely know.

'Okay?' Marco says when I catch up. He's standing behind an iron door.

I am so not okay. I glance back towards the empty street. The cab's gone. I take a deep breath. It's best to get my feelings about this out on the table. 'I…'

He raps hard on the metal door; the sound ricochets off into the night.

'I just f-feel...' I stutter, needing to stop for another breath, trying desperately to grab hold of a little courage. He's my new boss, and what with the audition bungle...

Marco raps on the door again, loudly, causing me to practically jump out of my skin. I feel myself stepping away from the door. What with the burglary, the missing admin, the fact I'm here looking for this mystery singer – looking for myself. I take another step back as Marco raps again, even louder this time. Then there's the clown convention dress fiasco. I look down at my shirt dress, pulling it gently over my knees. I now hate this dress. Again, he raps. I clutch my stomach, feeling sick. Can I tell him I'm feeling sick? That's an idea. I could go home. I could...

'Nelly,' Marco shouts at the metal door. 'Open up.'

I cringe. He's actually shouting now. Everything about him says desperately seeking illegal substances. I may have thought he was attractive before, but now the only thing I want to do is run. Turn tail and run fast, but it's too late. The door pulls back. Standing on the other side is a man with Afro hair and a thin, dark face. He's wearing a forest-green velvet jacket and some kind of ... I peer closer. What even is that? A purple paisley cravat. And then there's the jewellery. The man has more gold than a lost-at-sea Spanish galleon. Speaking of lost, now I seriously want to run. From the way he's dressed, he must be high up in the drugs trade. I take a step back.

'Oh for goodness' sake, darlings,' the man called Nelly drawls. 'Have you no patience?'

He gives Marco a withering look before returning his dark, wide eyes to me. 'So what have we here?'

'I'm–' I stutter.

'Hmm.' He draws himself in. 'An absolute walking fashion disaster.'

My mouth practically hits the floor.

'I see exactly what you mean, Marco. Thank you for the text. I needed a warning. Good God.' He pulls one bejewelled hand across his forehead in an exasperated fashion. 'This,' he waggles a hand in my general direction, 'is all eighties secretary vibe.' He throws both hands up in an attitude of total and unmitigated despair. 'I didn't know you could even buy clothes like this anymore unless you worked wardrobe for one of the networks. You were so right, Marco my friend. This is an absolute emergency.' He takes a step back.

I stand there, dumbfounded. Marco is staring at me. Nelly is staring at me. I don't like all this attention.

'The favours I have to do for you.' Nelly sighs. 'You just make sure that your next "voice of whatever" is wearing one of my gowns, or I swear I'll sue. This,' he points straight at me, 'is going to be difficult.'

'You got it, Nelly,' Marco says, glancing furtively back out into the street.

I wish someone would tell me what is going on. But Nelly looks like he's on the move. He's turning, throwing one skinny, velvet-clad arm up behind him in a circular motion. Inviting us to step over the iron grille at the base of the door before disappearing off into the darkness of his warehouse.

'I'm not sure...' I say, hurrying down corridor after corridor behind the two men.

'Just keep up,' Nelly calls back. 'You get lost in here, we may never find you again.'

I can believe that; the place is like a labyrinth, with a myriad of concrete tunnels and corridors interspersed with sliding metal doors. Where in the hell are we?

'Okay,' Nelly says, coming to an abrupt halt. 'This should do it. Cocktail, you said?' He glances back towards Marco.

Marco nods.

'Well.' Nelly leans in to the door, pulling it back and releasing the sound of the high-pitched sing of iron on castors. 'Anything you like?'

The door slides open. Nelly hits the lights, and now I am *seriously* dumbfounded because behind that industrial metal door is everything a girl could ever want for a night out. Sequins and tulles sparkle, intricate embroidery flowers up wide skirts, silk sleeves dangle from the bodices of flowing gowns waiting to be lifted and taken out for a dance. The place is packed to the brim with the most beautiful dresses I have ever seen outside of a magazine.

I gasp. Nelly looks over at me, trying to suppress a smile. 'Can I touch?' I say, raising one hesitant arm and indicating towards the row upon row of dresses.

Nelly takes my hand into his bony, ringed fingers. For a moment, I think he's going to shake it. Instead, he turns my hand over and looks at the palm.

'Clean. Yes.'

I feel relief well up inside me, imagining what he might think of my brother's hands. Thank goodness that particular habit doesn't run in the family!

'Touch, yes…' Nelly drawls, 'but don't tug.' He lets my hand drop back down.

'Absolutely,' I say, trying to hold back my excitement as I step into the room. I could spend an entire week in here, wallowing in all the beauty. I wander slowly towards the rails, running my hands gently across butter-smooth silks, liquid-cool satins, and encrustations of sequins. As I walk, I make a mental note never to introduce Nelly to my brother. He would never pass the hand test.

'Okay,' Marco says from behind me, still loitering in the door. 'I'll give you twenty minutes.'

I glance around. He's looking at his Rolex as though it's one of those cheap stopwatch things gym teachers used to have, and it's already counting down. The man has so little patience.

Nelly folds his green velvet arms across his large body. 'Certainly not. For that…' From a safe distance, he sweeps one arm over the length of my body. '…I'm not taking anything less than an hour.'

They're talking over my head, but seriously, I don't care. I'm with Nelly on this. Whatever he's offering, I'm going to take it.

'It's just a dress.' Unsurprisingly, Marco is sounding a tad like a grumpy toddler. I get the feeling he does that a lot.

Nelly crosses himself as though warding off a demonic spirit. 'Ugh, ugh. Don't you ever say that again. This,' he raises both hands around him as if summoning an orchestra, 'is a temple of fashion.'

Irritated, Marco clears his throat. 'Nelly mate, you've just got to zip her in.'

Despite my off-the-rack high-street fashion training, even I can see this is simply not the case. We're in couture country.

Nelly shoots Marco an irritated look. 'Even if that did accurately describe the process, which,' he sighs, 'it absolutely does not. What about the hair? The make-up?'

Nelly's got a point. I like to think I'm a bit of a whiz with the heated tongs, but what with the electricity cut and the lack of hot water, I hadn't had time to give myself a blow dry. I had thought the face was okay, though. I'd used my brother's arc lights in the garage so I could plaster something on. Maybe I went too far? Possibly *plaster* is just what I should have been avoiding.

'One hour.' Nelly's eyebrows pull into a perfect warning arch. 'Last offer, Marco. You can take my keys.' He slips his fingers around his waistband and pulls out a bundle of keys. 'Only no drinking, no speeding, and absolutely definitely no dogs.'

'Dogs?' Marco looks puzzled.

'House rules. The hairs get on the dresses.' Nelly shivers.

'Okay,' Marco says, shifting his weight and moving towards the door. That grumpy child attitude still hanging over his shoulders.

Nelly and I watch as he slumps through the hole in the wall that the sliding door has left.

Nelly puts his finger over his lips. His eyes darting mischievously as we listen to Marco retrace his steps down the corridor.

'Thank goodness.' Nelly breathes an exaggerated sigh of relief. 'I swear that man is half-ogre.'

I laugh. Trying to dismiss that awkward moment when I'd met Marco at reception and he'd matched my goblin perfectly with his more default ogre impression.

'Good.' Nelly nods in a smug, satisfied manner. 'This girl likes my humour. I can work with that. I think peacock-blue silk, a modern-faux Morris print. Maybe that trouser suit I finished last month. Nobody's seen it yet, and it's such a beauty.'

He slides his hands over my hips and waist. The gesture is totally unsexual. I can tell that for Nelly, I'm simply a mannequin. 'Yes,' he says, standing back, pleased with himself. 'Size twelve. That'll fit.'

MARCO

I drive away from Nelly's warehouse in his low-slung, banana-yellow Corvette Stingray. It's the Stingray that's growling, not me. Not yet anyway. Though the way I'm feeling, the car's tone matches my mood. I feel like an explosion in a bottle. That might come soon. Tonight was supposed to be simple – me and the new girl checking out some jazz joints. Uncharacteristically for me, I was even kind of looking forward to it. There's something about her, something that I can't quite put my finger on. She's different from the others, got a good head on her shoulders. She smiles most of the time, even when everything around her is crumbling. You get the feeling she can deal with it, pull it all around. But the dress? The outfit? The hair? Where the hell did she think we were going? It seems like nothing ever goes right in my life. Nothing's ever simple. Sitting behind the wheel of Nelly's overly flashy power car, a large part of me wants to just keep on driving – point the banana on wheels towards the motorway and keep heading away from the city till the fuel tank runs dry. Sometimes life, the responsibility of the company, the wrangling to make things work, it's all too much. Maybe Nelly should have added a few more things to that *do no*t list of his. Running the tank dry is never a good idea, and the car, despite being ridiculous, is Nelly's pride and joy. The car doesn't just growl; it screams *look at me now, go on, people, look at me now.* That's Nelly all over. He's a guy that likes the limelight.

I can't remember a time when he wasn't in my life. I'd be the first to admit that we've got an unlikely friendship. Nelly is camp and funny and flamboyant, and me, well I'm certainly none of that. If people are being kind, they might describe me as reserved. If they're being honest, they would describe me more accurately as grumpy, taciturn, permanently irritated. I should have been in with the in-crowd at school. I was the natural fit – my dad had the dosh and the flashy image. Not playing sports is always a problem, but with my connections, that shouldn't have been insurmountable. The in-crowd like sport. I, however, liked my guitar. But still, that shouldn't have been a deal breaker. Only, the in-crowd is all about self-assurance. They're winners. They believe in themselves. Me, on the other hand, I didn't like who I was. My father may have been a big man, someone people looked up to, someone they followed in the papers, in all the it-crowd magazines, but I knew the truth. The guy was an arsehole. I wasn't playing his game. I didn't want to talk about him or my life outside of school, so I just stayed in my room at the ludicrously expensive boarding school I'd been exiled to, strumming my guitar, writing depressing songs, and dreaming of living in a trailer in the backwoods of America. No doubt there's someone in the backwoods of America dreaming of my life. That's the irony. You very rarely get the life that suits you.

It's unlikely I would have ended up being Nelly's friend if the school hadn't forced him on me. We shared a room in year seven. He was ostracised; I was ostracising myself. Initially, I didn't think it would work, but somehow, from the way the guy looked at life with the wonder of a newborn chick, finding marvels in the patterns it throws at a person, it did work. That kind of wonder, you can't keep fighting it. Not when the person you're banged up with is doing it every single day. So that was it, friends ever since. And now, every year, he dresses the company's winning voice. He gets publicity. We get a free dress. I get to spend a few pockets of time with him. It works.

I stop driving and pull into a lay-by. I've got forty minutes left before pick-up. In truth, I needed this time. Needed to think through the shitshow that I'd found myself in. I hadn't even thought about the CCTV footage. Then again, I had been drunk. I know things are bad with the business. I've been borrowing money at zero per cent interest, and now that's all changing. Interest rates were going sky high. I'd tried to block up some of the leaks. Betsy had brought in funds and so had Fitz. They could both afford to lose money. Only they didn't want to lose money. Who would? As a point of principle, Betsy never likes to lose, and Fitz, the more control she has over the company, the more control she has over me. Is that what she wants? Difficult to tell with Fitz, but what with the two women watching over my shoulder, it's getting claustrophobic. Anxiously, I draw my hands through my hair. I'm totally in a fix.

Then there are the guitars. They're collector's pieces – were Ed Sheeran's and Bob Dylan's. Early versions. And the only thing I care about in the whole building. I thought if I just grabbed them off the wall when this audition process was over, I could buy my way out of the business. Head to some tropical paradise where you only needed a little music to see you through. Write a few songs. Leave the business to Betsy and Fitz. Only now, I can't do that. Because now we're missing our winning voice. I reach into my pocket and open my wallet. The SD card with the missing beauty's voice on is inside. I hold it between my finger and thumb as if I somehow have her captured. This kind of voice, this quality, the originality of the arrangement, the natural, nuanced ease of the pace – this could save the business. Then I could sit on my beach with my guitar and know that everything back home is ticking along just fine. She's not just my songbird. This broad, whoever she might be, is my golden goose.

CLARA

Within minutes of Marco leaving, Nelly had me sitting on a stool in front of a show-girl bank of bulb-ringed mirrors, my hair held back from my face in a stretchy white Alice band.

'Nice bone structure,' he says as he loads a palmful of white face cream into his hand.

'Thank you?' I say uncertainly, more because it feels like I should know what he's talking about. Do I really have good bone structure? I thought that was just a Botox and cheekbone thing. I find myself staring intently at my reflection.

'I'm going to go heavier on the eyes to bring out the blue. A little flick of liner. False eyelashes.' He raises his eyes heavenward as if, what else. 'And… I've got this lovely coral lipstick, which I use on all my girls. It's kind of my signature for the year. I think that'll do the trick.'

He slides a stool underneath him, edges himself close to me, and begins to work. I try to turn around a little so I can see what's going on, but Nelly just laughs and pulls the seat around the other way.

'No peeking. We don't want to spoil the surprise.'

And so he paints, and we begin to talk. I tell him everything. Well, almost everything. How I wasn't supposed to even be working for Marco. How there was a mix-up with the audition tapes, and we're trying to find one single voice. I don't tell him that I may have left the door open, therefore instigating the current crisis, or that the girl we are searching for is me. It's way too complicated.

'Finding the right singer in this city.' Nelly raises one single eyebrow before dabbing a fine make-up brush into the deepest sparkly blue eye shadow imaginable. 'Marco may be wonderful,' Nelly says indulgently, 'but he's always been a bit of a knee-jerk reaction man.' He smiles. 'We went to school together. The sensible thing is to just go through all the admin. She'll be there somewhere.'

'Maybe…' I clear my throat awkwardly, hoping I don't sound guilty. 'I mean, there are gaps, and the processed files are lost, and I mean…' I fluster. 'The thing is, no one remembers hearing her sing, so maybe she's a friend of a friend.'

He nods, then shoots me what I swear is a meaningful glance. 'Well, now. Wouldn't that be the oddest of things? Someone is auditioning and they bring their roommate's tape in just for a laugh.' Nelly is clearly not buying that line.

I feel myself blush. I so don't want to blush. Why do I always do that? I need to change the subject. 'Fitz thought scouring the clubs would be a good idea.'

'Hmm.' He purses his lips slightly. I get the feeling he's not keen on Fitz.

'You know her?' I ask.

'She went to school with us, too. Very wealthy family. Like ridiculously wealthy. She's been kind of going out with Marco for ages. Forever.' Nelly raises his eyes as if this is all so boring.

I feel my smile drop; the forever girlfriend is so much worse than the casual fling with the shareholder girlfriend. I hope Nelly isn't picking up on my disappointment. Marco might as well be married.

'Honestly.' Nelly continues painting small, intricate strokes over my eyelashes with a miniscule brush. 'I don't think there's any physical relationship left between those two. My absolute, honest-to-God opinion…' He leans in towards me, pausing with his brush held high, itching to spill a little gossip. '…I think she only goes out with him because her parents approve.' He gives a brief tut before continuing to apply the shadow. 'Very difficult man, Fitz's father. Almost as bad as Marco's was. Old school. But now Marco and Fitz are even more tied together.' Nelly scoots a little closer, edging the brush around the bottom lid of my eye. 'Marco had to sell shares in his father's company. Fitz and Betsy bought them up. So, no doubt,' Nelly gives his brush an extra coat of blue, 'Marco is feeling pretty trapped right now.' Nelly suddenly stops, dead still. His eyes narrowing. 'Do you think he could have sabotaged this whole thing? That maybe he didn't want the auditions to be successful in the first place?'

It's an odd thought. When I first met Marco that day in the studios, he had been totally out of control. Absolutely in sabotage mode. 'But why?'

Nelly shrugs. 'Maybe the company's in debt. Marco feels snookered. It's never really been his style; all that responsibility. He wants to get out, so he intends to bring the whole thing crashing down around his ears.'

Could Nelly be right?

'In which case,' Nelly says, allowing himself a small, secretive smile. 'The voice you're looking for. Well, you certainly aren't going to find it in this town. Perhaps there is no missing songbird.'

It's an interesting theory, only I know for a fact Nelly's got it wrong.

'Voila.' Nelly jumps back and gives my chair a spin so that I'm facing the mirror. I cannot believe what he's done.

Yet again, I find myself gasping. 'I look amazing,' I say. Awestruck.

He hangs his head beside mine in the mirror. 'And this, my lovely Clara, is only just the start.'

❧

MARCO

Ten minutes before I have to get back, I turn the keys in the ignition, pointing the banana in the direction of home. It's a home that's not mine. But isn't home the place where you're always welcome? So maybe, I guess, there's a bit of me that resides there with Nelly.

I park the car in the alley at the back of the building and fiddle through Nelly's keychain till I come to the electronic garage fob and give it a good press. The door slides open on its rails.

'Okay, Nelly,' I shout as I swing through the door to his inner sanctum. 'You've had your hour. We've got…' Words fail me, because walking towards me is the most beautiful woman I've ever seen in my life. The hair is perfect, the body is wrapped in this jumpsuit, it's all blue and purple and paisley. Understated but absolute class. Just, wow.

She smiles at me with these lush coral lips and it's like a sunburst coming out from behind a cloud. 'Hey, you,' she asks with a degree of confidence that I haven't seen in her before, 'what do you think?'

I seriously don't know what to say, so I just stand there dumbstruck for a moment before managing an awkward, gruff 'Hi' in return and totally avoiding the question.

She smiles again and takes a step closer to me, looking into my eyes with such intensity that I feel like something inside me is melting away. We stare into each other's souls. Moving slowly towards each other, hypnotised as sleepwalkers, one step at a time till we are almost touching.

'So, yeah,' Nelly breaks in, a note of confusion to his voice. 'I think she scrubs up okay.'

I couldn't agree more. I reach out to take her hand, then pull back as if I've been stung. I am not my father. I will not take advantage of people who work for me. Shit! Why did I get her to sign that contract?

Confused, she glances down awkwardly at her hand.

Luckily, Nelly is there as always with something light and acceptable to break the mood. 'Just don't get ketchup on the suit,' he says wryly, dusting her shoulders down as if she's a doll.

'Ketchup!' Clara laughs, the intense moment shattered.

'Oh, yes,' Nelly says, his features pulled into a serious frown. 'That guy might look like class.' He points one long finger towards me. 'But his tastes are positively pedestrian. Speaking of which, I called you a cab. She can't walk in those.'

We all glance down at the steeple-high, diamanté encrusted sandals that Clara's wearing before Nelly pushes past and slides open the door. 'Give my love to King,' he says brightly. 'Tell him he still owes me a bottle of Dom P for that nightmare of a woman he sent my way last month.' Nelly raises his eyes and shivers. 'I had to practically use scaffolding on the poor blob.' He grabs Clara's hand gently between his own. 'Not so for this little one, I tell you. She is an absolute keeper.'

'Oh, we're not...' My voice clashes with Clara's. She's also protesting, which makes me feel curiously hurt – what's wrong with me?

Seeing the confusion, Nelly laughs, glinting a mischievous look towards us and placing both hands in an attitude of secrecy across his chest. 'Course not. Okay.' He sighs. 'Fairy tale done.' He flicks his hands towards us. 'Shoo, shoo, people. Have fun.' He blows us a kiss before manhandling us out of the door and sliding it shut behind us.

CHAPTER 11

CLARA

The walls are black and adorned with framed portraits of jazz legends and magazine-worthy young men wearing the slickest, trendiest suits. Whereas Nelly's world was all fashion and flounce, this world is totally male. King looks like some kind of gangster lord with skin that has the appearance of chewed leather. His fingers are overly large, as if muscled by piano playing, and adorned with gold signet rings the size of dinner plates. Well, okay, not that big, but big enough. The man must be nearing seventy, but has so much hair sprouting out from the top of his wide, square head, it's surely got to be a wig. In one hand, he holds a tilted tumbler of whisky. Someone, somewhere, is apparently fixing Marco and me drinks. No one asked what we wanted. King simply told us we'd love the night's special. So, the special it is. I'm truly not fussed, anything that calms my nerves works just fine. In contrast, King doesn't appear to have nerves. He's rock steady. Just like his office, the man is immaculate. His black shoes polished to within an inch of mirror-glaze perfection. His unbuttoned shirt hangs open slightly. But, in a way, that looks so totally cool and smart that you wonder why everyone isn't doing exactly the same thing.

Even his tie is casual and cool, knotted and thrown over one shoulder. Worn there purposely? Or forgotten? Who would know? It all just looks fab.

I'm not feeling so cool even though the outfit Nelly fixed for me is absolutely gorgeous, and my make-up has never looked better. I didn't even know it was possible to look this good. I should be feeling a million dollars confident, only there's a big cringeworthy problem looming over the evening. I know that any minute, my pre-recorded voice is going to come warbling out of King's speakers, and I'm going to want the world to swallow me up. So, I'm perched on a red velvet banquette opposite King, hoping we can just get this over with really quickly and that someone is going to push a margarita into my hand to help me through the process. What's perhaps even more surprising is that Marco is not exactly looking cool, calm and collected himself. He's pacing. I guess there's a lot at stake for him. Sure, I can go through all the auditions and try to match the voice, but of course, I know that's never going to work.

King stops tapping his fingers the moment my Donna Summer number slices through the air. I don't even dare to breathe. Not one of us says anything as the track plays out, even Marco stops his pacing. Afterwards, for such a long, awkward moment, nobody speaks.

'So?' Marco says eagerly. 'Do you know who it is?'

King leans back in his chair, eyes closed, a slow smile spreading across his lips. My heart pounds as I see an odd expression dawning over that wrinkled seen-it-all, done-it-all face. The expression is clear – what he's heard is something special.

'I have no idea,' he murmurs, amazement dripping from every word. 'This voice, it's like nothing I've ever heard before.' He shoots Marco an amused look. 'So go on then, who is she?'

Marco shakes his head. 'We don't know.'

Marco had already told him this, but I figure King thought Marco was just playing with him.

King looks surprised at the revelation, finally taking it in. One of those gnarled hands reaches up to rub the equally gnarled face. 'I don't understand. She auditioned for you?'

Hmmm, King has a point. The situation is pretty confusing.

Marco looks sheepish. 'We…' he tries, as though suddenly realising this is an awkward situation.

We have fobbed off the press, but no one outside of the office knows the full extent of the disaster.

'The studio was broken into,' I say. 'Some of the audition materials were… They've been mislaid.' The burglary has to be a need-to-know basis.

Marco nods eagerly. 'Exactly. So we have this tape. She's the vocalist we want, and we're just trying to find a reconnect.'

King leans forward, opens a small wooden box on his desk and takes out a cigar. 'Well, I have to say, that is most definitely some voice.' He laughs, reaches down to a drawer, slides it open and takes out a pair of cigar clippers. 'You'll have to excuse me,' he says. 'This is cause for a celebration. I hear a lot of singers, but it's been years since I've heard anything that good, that original. I think you've found your winner.'

Marco sighs, starting to pace once again. 'Yes, but who is she?'

King raises one large, bushy eyebrow, a sparkle flitting over his eyes. 'That I can't tell you, but when you find her, you call me. Now…' he says, getting to his feet, 'where are those drinks?'

Once Marco and I are cocooned in the nightclub, King takes his leave. We're sitting in one of the best booths the place has to offer. Close to the dance floor but slightly raised so the sound doesn't blast us, and we can maintain a good look at all the artists. Despite what I told my brother, this could be a long night.

MARCO

Normally, this is exactly where I'd want to be. Only tonight, I'm feeling a seriously confusing mix of emotions. Part of running a record label, the part I love, means you're continually on the lookout for the next new thing, the next sensation. If you don't grab them quick, someone else will. I also have a demo tape sporting the most amazing vocals, yet I have no idea who this woman is or where she might be. This should be doing my head in, but all the angst I should be feeling about work, well, it just isn't there. Instead, my thoughts are focused elsewhere as I happen to be sitting opposite the most beautiful woman I've ever met.

'So.' She stirs her drink. 'That was a waste of time.'

Waste of time, seriously? Maybe she doesn't like being with me? Maybe I'm a waste of her time. Of course, she probably has a boyfriend stashed away at home, watching the clock.

'Sorry,' I say. 'I hope you didn't have plans tonight.' I start to fish. I can't help myself. 'Is there someone waiting up for you at home?'

Her face sours a little. 'Is it okay if we don't talk about home?'

So, there is someone waiting for her. Then she does this really odd thing: she rubs her hands like there's some kind of grease on them.

'Sure,' I say with a degree of nonchalance an actor would be proud of. 'Whatever.' I pretend to glance out at the stage. I mean I do glance, but I'm not really taking anything in, it's all just part of my act.

'It hasn't been a total waste, has it?' She sounds nervous. 'I mean, I enjoy being together.'

'Together?' I ask, shooting her a look.

'Here,' she says, her shoulders rising.

'Sure,' I say gruffly. 'You're a good worker.' I try to go for everything being ship-shape and businesslike. 'Pretty good in a tight situation.' Is that a compliment? I'm not sure. Luckily, she laughs. I've noticed she laughs a lot. I'm not sure if she laughs at all my jokes because I'm funny or because I'm the boss. This is a thought that's totally doing my head in. I know I'm insecure. They described me last year in the paper as a great catch. Seriously, that's what they said. Me and some film star who did a TV series set in space, and another guy who's a smug tech billionaire. Three of us, in the entire country, were voted the hottest males in the UK. Only, I don't want to be a great catch. I don't want the shadow of my father and his company walking into the room before me and colouring everyone's expectations. I don't want people laughing at my jokes if I'm not funny. Currently, I'm a stone's throw away from freedom. If I can find the woman singing on the tape, I can pull the company back from the brink and make my exit, then I can just be a normal guy, someone who's judged only for being themselves.

'You have such a wonderful life,' Clara says.

She's clearly a gold digger. Of course she is, that's what all the laughter is about.

'All the time Nelly spent on me...' She glances down at her outfit.

Yup, a gold digger with expensive fashion tastes. I make a mental note not to let her have the company credit card. Not even for a coffee run. 'He owes me a favour,' I say too sharply.

'Yes, but...'

Why is she smiling all the time? How can anyone be that happy and look that delighted. I must be scowling because suddenly her face falls.

'Do I look okay?'

'No.' I rein myself in. 'No, sorry, yes.' I correct myself like a tongue-tied idiot.

She laughs.

Clearly a gold digger, that last line wasn't even trying to be funny. Although, let's face it, I am used to people being chummy with me because of my money. It doesn't necessarily mean that she's a bad person.

I shoot her an appreciative glance. 'Well, Nelly's attention hasn't been a waste of time. You look great.' I'm big enough to be able to admit that.

She smiles a broad, open smile. My God, how easy it must be being inside her head. 'Thank you,' she says, still beaming.

In fact, she looks so much more than great. I'd like nothing more than to jump in a cab, head back home, and throw her onto my bed. Literally throw her, the whole caveman thing. Sod romance. This feeling is physical. Physical at its most basic, most immediate, most need-to-be-satisfied level. I don't say any of that, though, of course. She works for me. I have to rein this in. So, instead, I manage to divert the dialogue to the job in hand – finding our mystery woman.

'Hopefully, King will keep an ear out. He knows people.'

The sooner our songbird is found, the sooner I can get on with the life I want to live rather than being tied into the family company. Having people hanging off my every word, smiling at me like I'm a genius and laughing at all my jokes. If I wasn't the boss, if she didn't work for me, then I could ask her out, and maybe, who knows, just maybe it would work.

'King's quite a character,' she says lightly.

'He certainly is.'

'And...' Her eyes open wide in excitement, like some kid in a candy store. 'These cocktails,' she gasps. 'They are incredible.' She even goes on to swizzle her ice cubes with one long nail. She has lovely nails. Not just the sort for ice cube swizzling. I would love them running over my body. Running over every inch. 'Did you get the same?'

I remind myself quickly that she (thankfully) has no idea what is going on in my poor tortured, bestial brain.

We're talking about drinks, not bed. I shake my head. 'King

has this thing. He says he can match the cocktail to the person. He claims he knows exactly what you want before you do.'

She smiles. 'That's funny.'

I'm not sure it is, but I say nothing.

'Can I have a taste then?' She pushes one slim arm towards my glass.

Hmm, now I'm in a fix. I don't do the whole sharing saliva thing. It's one of my golden rules. Not even with Fitz, and we've shared just about everything else. Even boxer shorts. I've known Fitz for way too long, but even as this is racing around my brain, I feel my own arm handing the drink to her with a 'Sure, help yourself.' God, I'm such an idiot.

I feel a wave of irritation. What happened to standards? She takes my tumbler and pulls it towards her, pushing the straw to one side so she can press her pink coral lips against my glass.

'Oh.' She wrinkles her nose. 'That is so sour.' Suddenly, her expression drops. 'I mean, the drink is sour, not that you are… You're not.' Awkwardly, she glances back towards King's office. 'I mean to say,' she flusters awkwardly, 'I'm not saying Mr King thinks that you're sour.'

I can't help it; I throw back my head and laugh. 'I am! Actually, sour kind of sums me up.'

'No,' she says, reaching her soft hand out towards my wrist. 'No, not at all. You've got a lot on your mind.'

Escape, I think. All I'm ever really thinking about is escape. I find myself bending the corner of a coaster. A nervous tick. Embarrassed, I slide the thing flat.

'Sour, it's just… the way I am. Take it or leave it.' I shrug, immediately wishing I hadn't said that. I mean, who in their right mind would get involved with someone who's a self-confessed sour person, even with the cash/lifestyle incentives?

Clara flinches slightly. 'I don't know.' She slides my drink back across the table and removes her hand from my wrist. 'You talk like you're fixed in place. As though you have no choices. I think you're…' Her eyes widen and her pink lips part. For a breathless moment, I think she'll close the distance between us, lean in, and kiss me. But then, irritatingly, she sits back, glances away. 'Sorry, I'm just–'

'Not a therapist? Shame, most people are willing to try on the role.'

'No.' She smiles. 'Therapy is not my thing. You're funny.' She glances down at her pantsuit. 'I'm just a plain old receptionist. Not even a degree to my name.'

'Maybe I like the way you are.' I could kick myself. The compliment was out of my mouth before I'd had a chance to stop it. It's just the sort of smarmy crap I can imagine my father saying. The sort of lines he used to get women into bed. Instantly, I'm so mad with myself that I can barely talk.

The silence stretches, awkward and strained between us. I should write a book: *How to Kill an Evening in Two Seconds Flat*. I stare awkwardly around the room like everyone else in here is so much more fascinating than us, than her. Clara takes the opportunity to study the candle flickering on the dark, polished wood between us. But I can't help noticing that her shoulders are raised and that bright little spark of joy she gets in her eyes, well, that's gone. I'm such an idiot. I'm seriously aching to reach across the table and take her hand; to tell her that I'd like her to be more than just my receptionist. But I made a deal with myself. I don't mess with the staff. I am not my father. Not the kind of idiot who charms women into his bed with hollow promises, pretty lies, and a bag full of keep-it-quiet dough. I won't take advantage of Clara, no matter how much I would like to.

'I should get home,' she says abruptly, standing and grabbing her jacket from the banquet. 'Early morning tomorrow.' There's a hint of irony to her tone and a forced lightness as, in contrast, I feel panic rising in my own chest. I don't want her to leave. I'd rather sit with her in excruciatingly awkward silence than go anywhere or do anything. Time is slipping away, the distance between us widening with every second.

'Don't go,' I say simply, and I even surprise myself with the quality of my voice. It sounds raw, open, honest.

Her body stills as she searches my face. 'Why not?'

Why not? A dozen reasons fly through my mind, but I grasp the one that matters most. 'I'm not done with you yet.' I'd meant it to sound honest and raw again. This time, though, I'm not sure. Not sure that I'm not coming off as arrogant and entitled instead.

A pink flush stains her cheeks. For a long moment, she just stands there, coat half on, watching me through those deep blue eyes.

Then she sits back down, her movements slow and deliberate. After placing her jacket once more on the velvet cushions, she folds her hands on the table. 'You're right,' she says softly. 'We're not done.'

A kind of ecstatic joy surges through me. I'm not my dad. This is genuine. The way I feel for her. It's all real, and she feels the same way. I'll sack her tomorrow. Then we can be together. I reach across the table, palm up in offering.

After a cruel heartbeat, she places her hand in mine.

We are seriously so not done.

But suddenly, the moment is lost. She snatches her hand back, eyes flashing. 'Sorry, sorry. That's not what I meant.' She blushes awkwardly. 'I-I meant…' she stutters, standing again, shoving her arms into her coat. 'We're not done professionally. We still have a job to do, remember? The auditions. The missing…' She raises her eyes as if in irony. 'Missing songbird.'

My cheeks burn. Of course. It's work. Just work. That's her sole interest, and I admire her for that. In a way. It's an admirable thing. Besides, I can't even sack her now. If I did, she would most likely haul me into HR with a charge of improper advances, and they were, I was. She could probably sue me.

She looks away, jaw clenched. When she speaks again, her

voice is tight. Most likely it's being choked with hate and repulsion for me, her boss. I've over-stepped. She must think I'm a predatory idiot. Damn.

'Goodnight, Mr Delagado.'

Mr?

With that she strides off, not even waiting for a reply. I drop my useless head into my hands. I should have waited.

'Hmm.' I turn to see King standing behind me. 'That didn't exactly go well.'

'It was a business meeting,' I say, grabbing my own jacket. I've ruined everything. Pushed too hard, too fast. Just like my father.

'If you say so.' King leans against the booth. 'But I hope you'll permit me to offer this small observation – you are one crap businessman.'

He has no idea how right he is.

CHAPTER 12

CLARA

The midday sun beats on the pavement as I rush through the busy street towards Nelly's warehouse, the low heels of my sensible work shoes clicking hard against the concrete. I tighten my grip on the garment bag containing the pantsuit Nelly lent me last night. I'm desperate to get the thing back. It probably cost more than a year's wages. I can't afford to have anything bad happen to it, and the way my house operates, mishaps are par for the course. Although it's autumn, the sun is bright and low, shining directly into my eyes, which are dog-tired. I was up late last night – what a disaster, and I turned up at work early today, pretending to find the missing songbird. Which is clearly not going to be possible if I stick to working through the mound of recordings from the two-week audition stint. There is nothing so depressing as doing a job that simply doesn't need to be done. I'd also been pestering Stan all morning. I kept leaving him messages about the CCTV tape. I need to get to it before Marco sees it. I'm guessing the police can't have got hold of it yet. As soon as they do, they'll be hauling me in for questioning.

Then there was the club last night. My cheeks burn at the

memory. What even happened there? I am so confused. I'm getting such mixed signals. I know what I would love to happen. I would dearly love for Marco to wrap those wide, strong arms around me and pull me in for a kiss, but I'm not even convinced he likes me. Oh, that needs a correction. He does like me, as long as I'm manning a stationery cupboard or organising an office. If he knew the trouble I'd got him into, I'd be out of a job.

The thick metal door of Nelly's warehouse creaks open, blasting me with a welcome gust of air conditioning. 'Clara, darling!' Nelly emerges from behind a rack of gowns, arms outstretched. 'How was the ball? Did Prince Charming sweep you off your feet?'

I look blankly. Does Nelly know something? He can't. 'Prince Charming? Ball?'

Nelly waves his hands dismissively through the air. 'Figure of speech. Don't mind old Nelly.' He fixes on me with his wide brown eyes. 'How was the evening? Is the outfit intact? And Marco? Did he behave?'

'Perfect, gent,' I say, handing him the garment bag. 'The outfit's fine, not one spillage.'

'Good to hear.' Nelly hangs it on a rail.

'As for Marco, it's just a work thing. Purely professional.'

Nelly tuts, ushering me to a plush velvet stool. 'Such a disappointment. I had hoped there might actually be a pulse underneath those flashy cufflinks of his. It certainly isn't beating for Fitz.'

'He's my boss, Nelly,' I say firmly. 'It's just business. And despite you being so dismissive about him and Fitz, there is some kind of relationship there.'

Nelly squeezes my shoulder; sympathy etched into his brow. 'You say that to yourself enough times, you just might end up believing it.' He drops his lips to my ear. 'Not me, though. I can see you're carrying a torch for him.'

I sink further down onto my stool. 'Is it really that obvious?'

Nelly raises one eyebrow. 'To anyone with half a brain.'

My breath shoots in an uneven gulp of panic down my throat. 'Do you think he knows?'

'No.' Nelly shrugs. 'It's the half-a-brain thing.'

My mouth drops aghast.

'Teasing, teasing,' Nelly says, waving the comment away. 'But bless him, he's not very good at picking up the signs.'

'And there's Fitz,' I remind him yet again.

And once again, Nelly waves away the comment. 'I keep telling you. Despite all evidence to the contrary. That is not a thing. Marco is complex. I blame his father.'

'Isn't it normally the mother that gets the stick?'

Nelly winks at me. 'I like you. You're funny.' He takes my pantsuit out of the bag and begins to check it over. 'His father was a king in business. Uber successful in life. He had the kind of Master of the Universe face that all the billboards loved. Seriously.' Nelly stops for a moment, garments draped over his arms. 'It was like *Big Brother*. The man was everywhere. Marco was always seen as "the son", never as Marco. And…' Nelly hangs my borrowed pantsuit on another rack. 'Then there were the women. There were a lot of women. People took him to court, but…' Nelly shrugs. 'It all got hushed up.'

I can't help wondering if Marco isn't perhaps a chip off the old block. It really felt like he was making a play for me last night. Or, actually, was that me making a play for him? Grrrrr, why is this all so confusing?

'Marco just needs someone to fall for,' Nelly says wistfully.

Well, that's not going to be me. If I ever manage to amount to anything in Marco's mind, it would simply be the light entertainment. The hors d'oeuvres before the main course, an amuse-bouche. Besides, when he finds out I left that door open, he'll be giving me my P45.

'I'm thinking maybe I'll quit work,' I say, picking up a basket of coloured silks.

'Hmm.' Nelly looks at me quizzically. 'Haven't you only just started?'

'It looks bad?'

'It looks terrible.' He laughs. 'They'll probably think you were behind the break-in if you leave now.'

I feel my face go a bright shade of pink. Luckily, Nelly is deeply involved in a silk halterneck. 'Leave it six months,' he says casually, 'then hand your notice in.'

'I'm not sure I can do six months.' It's true, the stress of falling for Marco, covering my mess up with the locked door to the studio, and the fact I'm currently involved in a search for myself is doing my head in.

Suddenly, Nelly stops in his tracks. 'My, something is truly eating you.' He puts one hand on my shoulder reassuringly. 'Then yes, hand your notice in. Handwritten or typed? Help yourself to materials. There are envelopes behind that desk there.' He points towards a long, narrow white tongue of design engineering.

'Seriously?'

Nelly takes my chin in his hand. 'Absolutely, Clara baby. Life is too short.'

Nelly's right. Life can change direction in the flutter of an eyelash. I know that all too well from my parents. I should hand my notice in before I get a criminal conviction for breaking and entering, along with aiding and abetting the burglars and running a songbird hoax. It all sounds so bad!

'Handwritten, do you think?' I ask nervously.

'There's a lovely sense of raw honesty about handwritten,' Nelly says appreciatively. 'In the drawer, pens and paper.' He nods towards the desk again. 'I like the pink for a resignation. It adds that subliminal element of sorrow. But up to you.'

I stand up and trudge over to the desk.

'I always think white is a little funereal. Yellow has to be to do with sickness. You can't really beat pink. But…' He waves one arm dismissively. 'Don't overthink it.' He smiles at me. 'You'll need a drink. I'll get you a tea.'

Left alone in the showroom, I slide open the desk. Nelly's right; he's clearly a stationery lover. He has more than enough writing paper in here to get the job done, in a rainbow of colours. I pull a light blue sheet from the drawer and help myself to a pen. Who should I address it to? Marco and Betsy? At the thought, I feel my shoulders rise. Betsy would enjoy it too much. Just Marco. Pressing the pen onto the expensive unlined paper, I am about to write when my phone buzzes. I stop. It's a distraction. I should just get on with this. It buzzes again. I stare at the screen. It's Stan. I hit the green button.

'Stan.'

'Yeah, sorry, Clara. I was in late this morning.'

'I know.' I lower my voice. 'It's about the CCTV footage from the burglary. Can you get it to me before–'

'It's gone,' Stan says, and my heart sinks.

'The police?'

'No. Mr Delagado insisted that they weren't involved.'

Hmm, that seems odd.

'So, who's got the footage?'

'Mr Delagado.'

Nothing about this is stacking up.

'Stan, when did it get handed over?'

'Hmm.' There's a brief pause. 'Yesterday, I think.'

Yesterday! Yesterday? Then Marco must have seen me on it. Seen me going into the recording studio. If he did, he would have put two and two together. He'd know I'm the missing voice. So why hasn't he confronted me about it?

'You okay?' Stan asks from the end of the line, and I realise I've let the conversation go dead.

'Sure,' I say lightly. 'Of course, Stan. That works.'

Only it seriously doesn't.

❧

MARCO

It's still sitting on my desk. I have no intention of looking through it. Why would I? I'm just going to see my drunken self staggering back through the building late at night and lifting two valuable guitars off the wall. Did I honestly think I wouldn't get caught? How drunk was I? Okay, so I know the answer to that – no-sense-of-judgement drunk. What an idiot.

Betsy leans her head around the doorway. 'Where's the new girl?'

I don't want to think about the new girl. Not after last night. 'Lunch,' I say snappily. Hoping Betsy will disappear, I don't look up, but I can tell she's going nowhere, just loitering in the doorway looking for answers.

'And?' I say.

'Last night, did King know anything about our little Miss Golden Vocal Cords?'

'No. He was impressed, though.'

Betsy laughs. 'That doesn't get us any further. And the new girl, she's gone through all the original auditions? The unlogged pile?'

'Yup.' Betsy is beginning to irritate me. 'You can always check them yourself if you fancy.'

She gives me a sour smile. 'Not really my job.'

'No,' I say. I'm actually convinced that Betsy's job is purely to irritate me. 'Besides, both Terry and Jeff swear they can't remember auditioning the mystery woman and they say, with a voice like that, they would have remembered.'

'And you?' Betsy asks, her eyes narrowing. 'Would you have remembered?'

I'm guessing this is some kind of dig. Most people know I was pretty paralytic by the time the auditions were winding to a close. Adele could have come into the audition and I would have forgotten all about it. It was that bad.

'Sorry, Betsy,' I say, keeping my voice steady. Going for the moral high ground. 'What are you trying to get at here?'

She sighs, moving into my office. 'This company used to have a bit of a…' She hesitates. 'Reputation.'

'The best label in the country. I know.'

'Actually.' She draws her arms up, folding them in front of her. 'That's not what I meant. I meant the other thing.' She lowers her voice and leans in. 'Your father.'

'You do know he's dead, right?'

She purses her lips, a hard look deepening her already granite features. 'Don't get clever with me, Marco. Women were offered… Let's call it advancements or incentives. They were offered things in return for their…' she lowers her voice and leans in towards me, '…favours.'

She has seriously lost me now. 'You're going to have to just spit it out.'

Betsy steps forward, leaning her upper body across my desk. The woman is built like a bulldog. I have no idea what she's up to, but I sure as hell don't like it.

'How about if you carried out your own auditions? Snuck back up here with some young hopeful. Recorded it. Meant to get rid of the recording, but…'

'Seriously?' This is total utter BS. But I can't help myself. I feel my face flush with anger. 'I'm not my father,' I say, my voice laced with irritation.

'Well, that's for sure.' Betsy pulls back.

'You can't…' I get to my feet.

'Hi, guys.' It's Fitz. It's about the first time in my life I've ever been overjoyed to see her. 'Oh,' she says cheekily. 'This looks serious. Is it shareholder stuff? Should we be in the meeting room?' She glances towards the room we normally use.

'Hey, Fitz,' I manage, with a lightness I am not feeling. 'I didn't know you were coming in.'

'Just.' She waves her hands in the air. 'You know, passing by. I thought you might be out to lunch.'

'Working,' I say, holding up the remains of a sandwich.

'Oh, poor you. No rest for the wicked.' She laughs.

Betsy shoots me a hard look. I match her right back.

'Any news on the missing voice?' Fitz asks brightly.

'No.' I sigh. 'King didn't recognise the vocalist.'

'Hmm.' Fitz looks thoughtful. 'Know what, there's the charity ball tonight. She could be there. They have artists performing in all the different rooms. Maybe about thirty.'

'That's an idea,' I say enthusiastically. Anything to get out of this place. 'We could go?'

'Well.' Fitz lounges in the doorway, pulling her body one way, then the other. 'Actually, I was going to see if you would go with someone else. I'm kind of busy.'

I have no idea what Fitz's 'busy' would involve. Most likely nail bars and yoga classes. It's certainly not something most people would recognise as rushed off their feet. Then again, she's kind of letting me off the hook. I like Fitz, maybe I even love her. Maybe, but we haven't had a physical relationship for around twelve months. She's more like a sister to me now. She seems to feel the same way too. What I can't work out is why she's still sticking close.

Fitz draws in a long, deep breath. 'Maybe that new girl? Maybe you could take her to the gala. She knows that missing voice thing inside out.' Suddenly, Fitz glances around, scanning the suite. 'Where is the new girl?'

'Lunch,' I say.

Fitz's lips narrow thoughtfully. 'Oh right, that's good. I mean, it's good that you haven't sacked her yet.' She rolls her eyes. 'That's always so… so boring. So, yeah. I guess if the new girl hasn't been sacked…' Fitz shrugs her shoulders. 'Why not take her?'

❧

CLARA

'How's that letter going?' Nelly puts a mug of tea in front of me. The tea is a work of art in itself – a china cup and saucer carrying the most detailed purple flourishes of flowers. There's also a small daisy-shaped biscuit on the side and a silver teaspoon.

'You always do everything so beautifully,' I say.

'Oh, stop.' Nelly taps my shoulder in a flirtatiously light manner. 'Or my head will swell and I'll fall over my feet. A man has to be a balanced creature.'

I'm not sure what he's talking about, but maybe all arty people shoot the breeze with a little more imagination than your average Joe.

'And the letter?' He stares down at the blank page. 'Oh, well, that's going well. It'll be all done by the time you're sixty-five. Perfect timing.'

I laugh. 'It's tough. It's the job I've always wanted, but–'

He waves his hands. 'Don't tell me. I can't do the split loyalty thing. You do what you think is best.' With that, his phone starts ringing. 'I'll just take this call. Why don't you see if you can think up a few more words while I'm at it.'

'Hello,' he says brightly into his handset. 'Nelly here.'

I stare back at the blank paper. Then I begin.

'Dear Mr Delagado,' I start, but am immediately interrupted.

'She's actually right here,' Nelly says to somebody at the end of the line. I glance over at him, his eyes burning into mine as if this is a three-way conversation. He taps the top of my letter and narrows his eyes. Of course, it's Marco. He's either watched the footage and is about to give me a grilling, or he's ringing to see if I can pick him up a BLT on my way back. The man has a lot to–

'The gala?' Nelly cuts into my thoughts. 'Tonight?'

The gala at the Beaumont? I've wanted to go there for years. It's the biggest event of the year. Cinderella-style glamour. Sometimes my brother and Tim do the valet parking, and they always come home with stories about just how wonderful it is. Then I check myself, bringing myself back down to earth. Knowing Mr Delagado, he probably needs me to pick up his suit from the dry cleaners.

'Would Clara like to go?' Nelly says slowly, clearly repeating the conversation he's having with Marco with an exaggerated sense of diction so there is no way in the world that I'll miss out one syllable.

'Seriously?' I hiss.

Nelly covers the phone. 'Seriously.'

I finger the edges of my letter. I could go to the gala tonight and then hand in my resignation in the morning. Marco clearly hasn't looked at the footage yet. It's unlikely the shit is going to hit the fan today. As all these thoughts whirl through my brain, Nelly continues his conversation with Marco.

'I think it's a brilliant idea,' Nelly enthuses. 'Truly, one of your best.' He rolls his eyes and mouths the words 'so needy' with an accompanying wrist flick before seamlessly picking up where he left off with Marco. 'There will be lots of artists. You might easily find your little lost songbird there.'

That's not going to happen. Besides, Marco doesn't need me to go to the gala with him. 'What about Fitz?' I hiss.

Nelly gives a quick nod of acknowledgement before talking into the phone again. 'And Fitz? You could take her?' He pauses for a moment, giving small sounds of agreement in the wake of Marco's words. 'Uh-huh. It was Fitz's suggestion? And she said you should take the new girl?' Nelly's eyes widen in triumph.

It would be a treat, wandering around those grand rooms, listening to all that fantastic music. But I can't do it, this whole relationship is a mess, built on a lie. I shake my head emphatically.

Nelly's eyes narrow, and he purses his lips in an irritated fashion. 'She's indisposed currently. Sorry, Marco.'

I lunge towards him and try to grab the phone from him. He raises it up in one of his silk-clad arms.

'Sorry, bad connection,' he shouts. 'Call you back.' With that, he clicks off the phone and shoots me a withering gaze. 'You need to go to this gala.'

'Ughh, Nelly.' I bury my head in my hands. 'I don't. This whole thing with Marco is way too complicated.'

Nelly throws his hands up in the air. 'Everything with that boy is complicated. But this will be fun. Go, Clara. You have to,' he cajoles.

'I can't,' I protest. 'What would I even wear?'

With that he bursts into loud laughter, extending out his arms and twirling around like a fairy queen. 'Honestly, girl?'

'The trouser suit from last night.'

He smiles with a mischievous charm. 'Oh, I think I can do better than that. Besides…' He grabs both of my hands into his. 'No one is wearing one of my dresses tonight. I need someone to do the honours, or all the socialites will forget me.'

I can't believe anyone would ever forget Nelly.

'Please,' he implores, batting his long, dark eyelashes. 'Just for me. You can hand in your resignation tomorrow. I'll help you write it. I'll even deliver the goddamn thing. Just this one favour.'

I hesitate. Nelly has nothing to do with the whole music industry mess-up, and I do owe him. After all, he lent me that trouser suit and took over an hour dolling me up. A treat I won't forget in my entire lifetime. Perhaps it wouldn't hurt to at least try the dress on. 'Fine,' I say at last. 'But I'm making no promises about attending the gala. You can slip the dress over my head, but if it doesn't work…'

'That's my girl,' Nelly says warmly, taking me into his arms. 'It is so going to work.'

'I should get back to the office,' I say, glancing at the door and already feeling guilty.

'Oh no you don't.' He grabs my hands between his. 'Somebody else can handle all of that office malarky.' He waves one arm dismissively. 'Whatever it is they do in that prison to sound. I need you here. We have…' He glances at his watch. 'Five hours.' He looks me over. 'For tonight's gig, I need the full five hours. You can meet your Prince Charmless there.'

I laugh. 'What would he say if he knew you called him that?'

Nelly smiles. 'Deep down, he's just a big softy who loves a joke. Now, no more energy on that. We have work to do. Come, come, come.'

I follow Nelly to the back room, where a dress is draped over a mannequin, a shimmering blast of floor-length tulle – the skirt has two layers, one in the palest powder blue, the other in a graduated deep green dropping towards the floor. A bodice of shimmering silk looks like liquid illuminated by the bright lights in Nelly's showroom. The plunging neckline accentuates a narrow waist encrusted by a tiny pattern of seed pearls. Despite myself, I gasp at the sight of it.

'I was hoping someone would wear it this year, but I got no offers,' Nelly says, leaning in the doorway, hand on the light switch. 'What do you think?'

I move into the room as if drawn by a magnet, reaching out to touch the fabric. The bodice melts under my eager fingers. 'It's beautiful,' I breathe.

'I thought you might regret that resignation if you saw the dress.' He smirks.

'It'll never fit,' I say sadly. 'That waist is tiny.'

He laughs. 'An illusion, darling. That's what couture is. We wrap you in promises and wishes. The dress holds so much of the shape.'

I gasp. 'I would so love to wear that.' I think I'm in love.

'So, for goodness' sake, go try the thing on!'

CHAPTER 13

CLARA

Nelly insists on dropping me off at the gala, but when he takes me by the hand and floats me out the back of his warehouse, I have to do a double-take. His idea of wheels is just about as cool as it gets. If my brother could see me getting into this, never mind the dress, he'd be all over the engine. 'Is that a Stingray?'

Nelly turns towards me, his face bemused. 'Hmm.'

'Wow,' I say. 'I am seriously impressed.'

'Right back at you. You have an eye for high-end motors?'

I stare him squarely in the eyes. 'Any kind of motor.' I've had the best kind of brotherly obsessive training.

'Make and model?' His eyes narrow.

'Chevrolet Corvette.' I pause, running my eyes over the body, the slashed air vents on the front panel, the sparkling multi-spoked wheel caps. '1964?'

He nods in heartfelt praise. 'So not just a pretty face.'

I laugh. 'Full of surprises,' I say as I swing the layers of cloud-like tulle that I'm wrapped in. 'But a bigger surprise might be how is all of this going to get into that.' The inside of the car is tiny. All streamlined.

'Don't you worry,' Nelly says breezily as he walks around to the passenger door and swings it open. 'I've been doing this a long time. Come, my lady, let me wrap you perfectly for presentation.'

It's a five-mile jaunt across town. I have to confess, I'm not as into cars as my brother but Nelly's Corvette is seriously cool, and luckily the traffic is kind to us – no sitting in jams. We're there in the blink of an eye.

'Thank you so much for everything, Nelly.' I gently touch the beautiful skirt, the one that's graduated and graded like an ocean, whilst holding me tightly and comfortably as a cocoon.

'My absolute delight, darling,' Nelly says, checking the rear-view mirror as he pulls into the line of expensive black limos that are heading under the wide awning of the Beaumont drive-through canopy. 'Just make sure, if anyone asks, you tell them you got it from Nelly's. Actually.' He wraps his hands against the steering wheel and shoots me a cheeky smile. 'Sod them asking, you tell them anyway.'

I place my hand over his and give it a squeeze. 'I will, Nelly, seriously, I will.'

He pulls on the handbrake. 'Well, go, girl, go.'

I lean over and plant a kiss on his forehead and his face crinkles in mock delight.

'Not my princess, princess. Go find that Prince Chumpworth.' He rubs my shoulder firmly. 'And remember, you don't have to be back by twelve.'

I wish that were true. My brother will be on my case if I haven't got a good excuse. Is this a good excuse? I glance out of the window, feeling like the world is at my feet.

'You better be quick,' Nelly says, staring out at the forecourt. 'That valet's itching to park me.'

I unbuckle my seat belt, grab my bag, glance out at the forecourt, and my jaw drops to the floor. Oh no. It's my brother's mate, Tim.

Tim's rushing towards us, wearing a peaked cap and a tight red jacket. Luckily, he's more interested in the car than he is in me. He's straight round to the driver's door.

'Fine. I'm fine,' Nelly says, holding up one decisive halt-style hand.

Tim's face caves in disappointment.

'Not stopping,' Nelly adds with a brief smile.

Neither am I. I open the car door and slip out. If Tim's here, my brother will be too. He might be able to cope with me working on the reception desk at Delagado Towers, but he wasn't keen about the upgrade to the seventeenth floor. He hates unpaid overtime, and he's always had a bee in his bonnet about the music industry. It was the trap that my parents got caught up in – the promise of fame, the overworked nights. Life with an empty fridge, with only enough money for pick-me-ups that you can all too easily get hooked on. I can't have Minty knowing what I'm up to.

'Great car,' I hear Tim say behind me as I pick up my skirts, angle my face towards the red carpet, and head for the large glass doors of the Beaumont.

'Hey!' I've walked smack bang into a growling tuxedoed man. I grab his jacket to steady myself.

'Sorry,' I say, cringing and glancing up from my diamond shoes.

'Clara!'

It's Marco. Marco Delagado is staring at me. Darkly handsome, wearing a well-tailored dinner jacket that fits so effortlessly it could easily be a second skin. His gaze travels the length of me in a way that makes me feel like a fairy princess wafted down from the heavens.

'You look…' he pauses, as if catching his breath, '…amazing.'

I can feel my smile lighting up my face. In fact, lighting me all over as if a beam is radiating from my body. Move over, Lady Liberty, no torch needed. I just shine.

Marco clears his throat awkwardly. 'Yeah, that Nelly, he could make a silk purse out of a pig's ear.'

My face falls.

'Oh, Mr Delagado?' a woman with a camera that's more lens than body calls out to Marco. 'Any news on the Voice of the Year?'

He turns to answer her whilst I hurry up the steps towards the door, feeling like a fool. Sure, I know the dress is gorgeous, Nelly is a genius. I know all of that, but… tears sting my eyes as I tumble towards the glass doors. I need the bathroom. I have to take a few minutes. Grab myself a few breaths. Stop feeling like I'm in a borrowed dress and have no right to be there. I'm here to work, I reassure myself. Suddenly, my arm is yanked gently back. If he thinks he can just say something like that, and then… I turn, and a surge of heat rushes to my cheeks because standing on the step below me, my elbow held gently in his hand, is Minty.

'Clara? What are you doing here?' His brow furrows as he takes in my floor-length gown and hair gloriously upswept with the pearl and tortoiseshell clips.

'I'm, um, I'm here for work,' I stammer.

'Dressed like that?' Minty gapes. Gently, he holds my arm and ushers me to the side, his face perplexed and hurt. 'Sis, have you got yourself mixed up in something dodgy?'

I glance behind me. In the foyer of the Beaumont there are banners advertising music awards. I cringe.

'No, it's just…'

'Escort work?' he says, still looking hurt.

'What!'

I glance down at the forecourt. Tim is still swooning after Nelly's disappearing taillights and Marco's spinning fairy tales to the press a 'so many great voices' kind of thing, stating that in such a talented year, it was difficult to judge.

'Cos escort work,' Minty continues, shaking his head, 'is just a small slip and slide to prostitution.'

'Minty!' That's clearly not true, but he is ridiculously overprotective, and okay, yes, he's led a sheltered life. It's not what he thinks, but how can I tell him the real reason I'm here? For Minty, the music industry is as bad. It chewed up our parents and spat them out.

'It's the choir,' I say with a blinding flash of inspiration. 'The choir's singing.'

'Ah.' Relief floods his features.

Minty will have no idea that the dress I'm wearing is couture and the pearls in my hair happen to be real.

'Of course.' He grins. Grins before he looks sheepish and awkward. 'That's great. I'm sorry, sis. Didn't mean to insinuate.'

I wave one hand dismissively; what's an accusation of prostitution between siblings? Nothing.

He sighs. 'Honestly, you would not believe the day I've had.' He glances around at all the fancy cars. He's clearly out of his comfort zone. With Minty, cars are normally cheap and cheerful. Something to be fixed. He's like a fish out of water with all these high-end vehicles. 'Sorry, didn't mean to…' he repeats.

Below us on the steps, Marco has finished talking to the press. He's smiling that wide confident, entitled smile that he seems able to switch on at will as he moves towards me, two steps at a time. Nelly's taillights have disappeared. Tim is about to turn, eager to find my brother and tell him all about the car.

'Got to go, Minty.' I clear my throat. 'Warm-ups.' And I bundle myself in a totally ungainly fashion, a fashion my dress absolutely does not deserve, through the wide gilt and glass door into the lobby.

MARCO

The limo inches forward in the traffic, hemmed in on all sides by paparazzi and fans – a lot of talent will be playing tonight. I just hope we can find ours. Instinctively, I tug at my collar as I offer up a silent curse to Fitz for forcing me into this penguin suit. The old one I had was just fine. This one is way too flashy, too sleek.

When the wheels of the car finally stop inching forward, and a host pulls open the door right beside the red carpet, a swell of shouts erupts from the waiting journos. A noise that makes me want to sink back into the safety of the limo and hightail it out of there. The attention is too much. Mostly, they want to find out about the auditions. We should have announced the winner by now, but there are other questions, too, like: 'How is the company holding up in the current financial crisis?' 'Is there really money in music anymore?' Do they know something? Possibly. It's difficult to keep anything quiet in this town. Along with questions I'd rather not answer, there's also the inane drivel that the media thinks up: 'What are my views on...?' In short, once that door is open, I'm met with a barrage of questions. The odd thing is, I'm not even convinced any of these people actually want answers. Well, maybe about the auditions. The whole country wants to know how we're doing with that. But the one thing I cannot do, under any circumstances, is let on to the world that there's any kind of a problem.

Cameras flash like a firing squad as I take my first steps along the red carpet. With the click, click, click, a familiar panic rises in my chest. I hate these events. The phoniness. The preening. The posturing. It's everything that's bad about the music business and the city arts scene. But Fitz was right, we need to show our faces, and perhaps our missing songbird is going to be here. Currently, finding that single voice is my best hope for freedom. If I can get her signed, I can leave the business on a good footing for Fitz and

Betsy, and they'll let me walk. There's no chance of walking out when the company is in chaos.

I summon up a cocky grin, lower my face in an ironic, barely interested attitude as, with one hand, I throw up a peace sign, eliciting another frenzied response from the crowd. I'm the bad boy of the music scene. They love me. I don't even have to try. All it takes is a father with a media-worthy reputation, a few drunken nights out on the town, and the adoption of a permanent scowl. Simple.

'Marco! Over here!' the wall of reporters shout, thrusting microphones towards me.

I wonder, fleetingly, if I could just run up the red carpet and lock myself behind the glass doors, turn that peace sign to reverse. Maybe not, but I'm sure as hell not going to talk to them. The auditions were such a full-on shitshow. I have absolutely nothing to say. Silence and moodiness are often the best defence.

Gloria, a platinum blonde from *The Times* with an upper body that defies gravity, shouts after me, 'Marco, Marco, how did the auditions go?'

I turn towards her. I'm not under any illusions. I know, as well as Betsy and Fitz, that we need these people. It's not just record sales that keep the company afloat; it's confidence. Confidence is key. So even though I might well flirt with the idea of ducking out, being unforgivingly rude and alienating the whole circus, I know I can't actually run and hide behind the glass doors of the Beaumont. This is work, and work pays the bills. Besides, I need to choose which shark to feed myself to, and Gloria is as good a beast as any. So, I turn towards her but keep walking backwards as I dish out an 'all good' with a wink.

More camera flashes. I feel someone grab my elbow. Blast. I turn, about to give whoever it is a mouthful. We all know the rules: the red carpet is an ask but don't touch kind of deal.

But I'm totally floored. 'Clara?'

Never mind the flashbulbs of the press, my own eyes practically pop out of my head because this is not office Clara or even the woman I went out with last night. This Clara is a vision of beauty. She's wrapped in a wide spray of ocean-like fabric that tumbles out from a seriously perfect body. Her hair is on top of her head in a mass of intricate curls. She's like some kind of marine goddess. How is she even holding that dress on? Wow.

A camera flash blinds me for a second, and when my vision clears, she's smiling at me. Just me. Just her and me on that carpet, and she's close enough to touch, to smell. God does she smell good, citrusy and fresh. I open my mouth to tell her how gorgeous she's looking but all that comes out is a strangled, 'Uh...'

Smooth, Marco. Real smooth. I could kick myself.

Heat floods my cheeks. Idiot. I am such a... I take a deep breath, centre myself, then go for it again. 'Wow,' I say, then the worst backhanded compliment slides unchecked from my mouth. Something on the lines of 'Nelly outdid himself this time'. As soon as the words are out of my mouth, I bite down hard on my bottom lip. I've just given the total credit for this woman's beauty, to this woman's absolute glory, to my mate. I groan inwardly, my body slumping into its black-tie armour. She must think I'm a fool. Which I am. But something about this woman short circuits my usual charm and wit.

When the, whatever it was, came out of my mouth, I saw her face drop. Her whole bright-eyed expression destroyed. I want to reassure her, to say something to diffuse the insult, but the lights from the cameras are still pop, pop, popping, their lenses, broadcasting my awkward fumbling to the world. God, I hope the press didn't get my comment to her. What kind of range do those mics have? Mind you, if they did, I could listen back and find out exactly what it was that I said. I am such an idiot!

'The auditions, Marco?' I hear the platinum blonde from *The Times* whine. 'Come on. Can you give us a hint?'

To save face, I pivot from Clara. Greeting who I would

normally class as my foes – the press – with an affable grin. 'So much talent this year, it'll be tough to pick a winner. But…' I flash my eyes at the reporter. 'I think this year, we've found someone really special.'

'Oh?' Gloria smiles coquettishly back at me. 'Just a hint more?'

I take a step back down the red carpet towards her. I need a little more time. A moment to get my thoughts in order. Clara is seriously messing with my head.

'It's all under wraps,' I tell Gloria. 'Hush-hush.' I raise one finger to my lips. 'Big secret.'

Gloria nods conspiratorially. 'But you'll give me the first scoop,' she says, flashing her green eyes at me.

I dish her out some kind of BS, which is wrapped up in a lot of words but basically says absolutely nothing, before turning away, calm. My facial expression is smoothed out and muscled into something approaching the norm I'm going to need to get through the evening. So, in my case, that would be a half-scowl, half-smile. When I face Clara again, I've regained my composure – at least on the outside. But inside, my heart is racing because, for me, the red carpet just got a whole heap more interesting with this woman on it. Only… my face switches to full-on frown. Clara is standing at the top of the steps, looking awkward. Some guy with his back to me has her arm locked into his. He must be one of the valets – he's wearing the uniform – but there's an odd possessiveness about him, which makes my skin crawl. The situation is over quickly. She pulls away from him, but it's clear she's unsettled. An ex? I wonder. Or is it something more sinister? He did not look happy. But there's barely time to process. The guy has vanished into the crowd and she's on her way again, turning her back to me and the press and dashing through the door like a stick of dynamite thrown through a prison wall. What the hell was that all about?

❧

CLARA

I'm in the most beautiful dress in the world. My make-up is done within a millimetre of perfection. My hair is a work of art, and I'm sitting in a stall of the ladies' room, pinching hard on the palm of my hands in an attempt not to cry. What an idiot I am. Why am I leaving my heart open to this guy? He doesn't know how to treat anyone with respect. I'm disposable to him, less important than stationery. And I've seen what he does with that! I should go. If I text Minty, he'll take the night off, get a car, and drive me home. I'll tell him all about the job at Delagado Sounds, that I have signed a contract, so they weren't exploiting me, but actually I've decided to leave the company. Maybe music isn't the right industry for me after all, so there's absolutely no need to panic. Tomorrow I'm handing in my notice. What a first-class mess I've got myself into.

'No tears,' I hiss to myself. 'No tears.'

In the meantime, a sink-orientated conversation is striking up outside my stall.

'You look wonderful,' someone with a pinched nasal voice says.

'Don't we all?' comes the reply. 'You too. Love that bird you've got on your head.'

I can't help myself. I feel laughter bubbling up inside me.

'It's not real,' the nasal woman says defensively.

'Of course not,' the second woman gasps before lowering her voice. 'That woman with the lizard wrapped around her neck, though. I think the lizard's real.'

'Hmm,' the first woman says thoughtfully. 'That is so not PC.'

'Exactly. I mean, duh, the planet,' says the second woman, clearly enjoying being able to throw stones.

'How's that going?' the first person asks seriously.

'Still spinning,' comes the reply. 'Did you get here by jet?'

'Helicopter,' the first woman says. 'I won't be doing that again!'

'The planet?' the second woman asks.

'Oh, no, darling,' the first woman titters. 'My bird. It almost flew off.'

'Blades,' the second woman states with what sounds like a nodding understanding. 'So bad for the up-do.'

I take a deep breath. This seriously is a different world. Would it matter too much if, for my last night, I just have a little look and a quiet laugh? Tim and Minty would love the stories I could bring back. It's just one evening. What harm could it do?

❧

The grand ballroom of the Beaumont is truly dazzling, all crystal chandeliers and marble floors. Everyone should have this kind of fairy-tale experience once in their life. I stand in my amazing gown, twirling around in the vast foyer, looking up at the beautifully painted ceiling.

'Found you.'

I find myself bumping back to earth to see Marco standing behind me. He looks seriously gorgeous in that black tie and jacket, and he smells so clean – fresh from the shower rather than the garage like my wonderful brother and his mates. Despite the fact this man appears ever ready to fling an insult, my heart flutters. Seriously, it does, like a butterfly in a net trying to pull itself away from the trap. I know Marco Delagado spells trouble, but he is just mesmerising. His dark eyes search mine and I find myself never wanting the moment to stop.

'Look,' he says abruptly, 'I'm sorry. I didn't mean… I mean the carpet thing. My comment. You look… You look lovely. Nothing to do with Nelly. Everything to do with you,' he says, running a hand through his stylishly messy hair.

It's as if not one second has passed since we met on the red carpet of the Beaumont's steps. Space and time have collapsed into a single moment that is all about now, and I like this, especially when he follows it up with a: 'You're beautiful, Clara. Really beautiful.'

I feel the heat in my cheeks. 'Thank you.' I'm truly glowing, my heart rising so far in my chest I half expect it to grow a pair of wings and fly me off.

But I have to make some kind of reply. I'm not a child, so I shake one hand dismissively. 'It's all right about earlier,' I say. And then an odd thought strikes me, could he be nervous? Could that be why he keeps slipping up? The insults, the bossiness, is it all just bravado? I glance away as I feel that glow I had been feeling turning into a neon-bright flush, making me feel as self-conscious and floundering as a streaming flare shot into a dark sky. This entire relationship is hit and miss.

'No, it's not all right,' he mumbles, clearly irritated with himself. 'I apologise. Sadly, I can't help it; arsehole is kind of in my genes. It's in my veins.'

I laugh. I have no idea what's flowing through mine. Most likely motor oil.

'Forgiven,' I say with the easiest smile I've ever had to find. Because he is absolutely forgiven. I just want to be close to him, close to him for as much time as humanly possible. 'Besides, you were kind of right.' I run my hands over the weightless tulle web of my dress. It feels as though I'm wearing nothing but air. 'Nelly is amazing.'

'May I?' He smiles, offering me his arm.

'I think that you may, kind sir.' I even allow myself a little bow.

'We have work to do,' he says seriously.

My smile drops a little. Work. Looking for myself. Unfortunately, I can see all kinds of problems with that.

Luckily my mood doesn't stay short of euphoria for long. The

Beaumont is possibly the most beautiful hotel I have ever been to in my life or, indeed, in my dreams.

'Connaught Room first,' Marco says, lifting a glass of champagne from a waiter as we pass and pressing it into my hand. 'They have the best voices in there, closest to the foyer. If our mystery songbird is here, my bet is that's where we'll find her.'

That kind of goes without saying. The woman is going to be following us around all night, but poor Marco doesn't need to know that. His flat palm finds the small of my back, a casual intimacy that makes my pulse jump. One evening in heaven before it all comes crashing down. Is that too much to ask?

It's no wonder the best voices tend to be found in the Connaught Room. It's spectacular, a bejewelled treasure of a room. High stuccoed ceilings. Long golden mirrors. A gleaming wooden floor and packed to the brim with beautiful people. There's a gorgeous-looking woman in her late thirties about to take the mic. She has a full Afro and the kind of figure I, and most likely the majority of the other women in the room, would die for. This girl doesn't need couture. Strip her naked, and she'd look even better.

'This could be her,' Marco says eagerly. His eyes brightening in anticipation.

'Umm hmm,' I say, grabbing a bite-sized delight that just so happens to be sailing past on a silver tray – a sliver of raw beef with horseradish in a hat of fresh parsley. Delicious. I find myself wondering if there is any way I can sneak a couple home for Minty and Tim. No, maybe not. It's not quite the serious woman-about-town image I'm trying to cultivate. More the fugitive vibe which, once they discover it was me who left the door to the studio open, will fit me like a glove.

I turn back to the stage just as the young woman starts to sing, and she truly has the voice of an angel. Light but resonant, with this wonderful touch of clear funk laced through.

'She's great,' I whisper into Marco's ear. As my lips touch his skin, I feel my heart rise in my chest. Rise so completely, like a solid block of beating muscle, that for just a moment, it threatens to short-circuit my breathing. He rests one arm around me, encircling my naked shoulders. With this small, possibly casual, touch, every inch of my body fires into life.

'But she's not our girl,' he says simply.

In truth, I no longer care. I just want to stand there with him forever. Then I remember Fitz, and it's almost as if he can hear the thoughts circulating around my brain because he pulls away.

'I was just wondering...' I say as the room begins to buzz again with light conversation. I pull my top lip over my teeth, steeling my nerves. 'So, um... Fitz. Are you two–?'

'Oh, that's nothing,' he says firmly. Pulling away from me slightly. 'Force of habit. Parental pressure. We were kids. School kids when we er...'

I cringe at the er, hoping he can get through it quickly. Luckily, he does.

'I mean, we still see each other, but it's more like brother and sister.'

Being an only child, I doubt Marco has any idea what that's like. Besides, I can't help feeling there's a note of guilt in his eyes. Does Fitz think that's what they've got, some kind of sibling relationship? But it looks like I'm not going to get to the truth anytime soon, because the bugger goes for a conversation shift.

'And you?' he says, taking a step away and examining me curiously. 'Is there someone in your life?'

I laugh, shaking my head. 'No, not at all.'

There's a long, awkward moment. I have no idea what he's thinking, but something is certainly going on behind those dark eyes of his. Luckily, he breaks the mood.

'We should push on.' He glances out of the Connaught Room into the intricate labyrinth of passageways that the Beaumont is so famous for. 'Come.' He offers me his hand. 'Have you been here before?' he asks, as we step out of the room.

'No,' I say, managing to wangle in a note of surprise in my voice as though it's the oddest thing in the world that I haven't graced the hallowed halls of the Beaumont with my presence before whilst knowing full well that this hotel is well above my league.

'It was the Earl of Ashbourne's place before it was called the Beaumont. Have you heard of him?'

'I don't think so. Ashbourne?' I say, drawing out the name uncertainly. If it wasn't someone attached to the First World War, Second World War, Fire of London or the Black Death, my knowledge of historical figures and events is pretty slim.

'He was a notorious philanderer. Hence all the passageways. It's easy to get lost.'

I can see that Marco's right. The passageways seem identical but spin away endlessly in all directions. 'It's quite a place.'

'Yeah.'

I take a deep breath, knowing I should level with him a little. The idea of us hunting down a mysterious voice, one that he's already attached to, is just ludicrous. 'About this voice that you're looking for… Couldn't you just use someone else? That woman in the Connaught Room was amazing. Couldn't you just…?' There's a long pause, in which we continue to walk down one of the long corridors, and I can't help but feel there's something he's not telling me. Which I guess is kind of fine because there's a hell of a lot I'm not telling him – call me nosy, but I can't help but be curious.

He glances around him, lowers his voice, and leans in towards me. 'The company is not doing too well.'

I'm surprised at his honesty, but then remind myself that I work for him. I'd had to sign an NDA. But actually, it kind of all makes sense. The company used to be family owned. Times have changed. 'Hence the shareholders?'

'Exactly. I had to take people on. Oh, hang on a minute.' He stops, glances down a corridor to our right, and suddenly seems amused. 'If you haven't been here before, you have got to see this.'

Grabbing my hand, he hurries me down a corridor, the sounds of voices and music fading behind us.

'Are you sure we should just...?' I look nervously back over my shoulder.

'No. Honestly. This has to be seen to be believed. And hardly anybody knows it's here.'

So much for looking for that missing voice. I mean, I'm not too worried about that, anyway. Besides, I'm seriously enjoying the guided tour. Whatever the Earl of Ashbourne's motivations were, he certainly knew how to build a palace.

'Here,' Marco says, once we arrive in a large, white, empty room. At the far end is a row of what looks like floor-to-ceiling curtained windows.

'Here?'

Marco pushes forward.

I glance back over my shoulder, not convinced that we should even be here. It feels a bit backstage.

'Clara.' He reaches out his hand, and so much for resistance – I might as well have had a spell cast over my body. My own hand raises up towards his. I practically glide in his wake as he pushes open the doors at the back of the room and we find ourselves standing on an intricate wrought-iron balcony. One that's covered with trailing jasmine in full bloom.

'This is amazing,' I gasp. Below us is a small courtyard with a fountain. The place is barely lit, so the golden light from the hidden wall lamps bounces off the water, scattering the courtyard in a ripple of orange waves that dance across the walls.

'Isn't it? I love it up here. You can't actually get into the courtyard. This balcony has the only entrance.'

'A secret garden.' Enchanted, I lean over the balcony.

'Yeah.' He places his hand on the railing and it accidentally covers mine. The feelings that surge through my body are so intense that I gasp. 'Sorry.' He pulls back his hand. 'I'm so sorry.' He turns his face away from me.

'No,' I say, reaching out, placing my hand on the angle of his chin and moving his face back to mine. His gaze drops to my mouth, and my breath catches.

This can't happen. He's my boss, for God's sake. I lied to him about the songbird, I…

'Clara.' His hand rounds the tight silk of my waist, coming to rest on the small of my back. The sound of my heart beating bangs against my eardrums as he groans. 'You drive me mad. You know that?'

This is all happening too fast. Much too fast, but I don't care. I just want more – more of his touch. His skin against mine. The feeling that nothing matters but the two of us.

'I…' But before I can even respond, his lips are on mine, and the world dissolves into a whirlpool of passion as he pushes me back against the wall. My skirt is up, and I'm drowning in a sea of silk, tulle, and desire.

'We shouldn't,' he whispers.

Without a pause for thought, I reach up, grab his tie, and pull his face hard back towards my lips because we must. I let my hands, my arms, my body wrap itself around him. I've never been touched, or touched anyone else, like this before. Never felt this all-consuming swell of emotion and longing. My dress is around my hips as he hoists me up against the wall then pushes the bodice of my dress down on one side, exposing a breast, taking it briefly into his mouth before slamming into me. For one moment, the whole world stills, nothing matters, and nothing exists beyond the energy of our lust. I completely lose track of time. It's as if we're no longer living in the same world as before. Time has no meaning.

When we eventually break apart, breathless, Marco drags a hand through his hair, looking torn and confused. 'I shouldn't have. I… I'm so sorry.'

Sorry?

'No, I shouldn't.' He can barely look me in the eyes. 'It's not…'

I remember pulling his tie, forcing his lips onto mine. I can't believe we just did what we did. I feel a wave of embarrassment. Awkwardly, I brush down my dress. Tears prick my eyes. What came over me? The man is my boss. This is a public space. My brother is downstairs! Okay so not close downstairs, but he's within sprinting distance.

'It's…' he stutters. 'I can't help feeling… Shit.' He drags one hand through his now thoroughly messed hair, the hair that only moments before I had grasped hard between my fingers.

I'm going to cry. I know I'm going to cry. He's still blustering on, saying nothing. Not even looking at me.

'I can't help feeling…'

'A secret courtyard, you say?' A woman's voice filters through the empty room at the back of us. The same room that we walked through. Panic floods through me.

'Yes,' comes a male voice. 'Are you sure you haven't been here before?'

Marco's face pales. 'Shit.'

'Bugger!' I panic, desperately trying to rake my appearance back together.

'That's Fitz's parents.'

My entire world collapses.

'You stay here,' he says, straightening his tie, brushing down the shoulders of his jacket. 'I'll get rid of them.'

'But…' Whatever I was going to say dries on my tongue because Marco is not waiting. This is clearly too important for him. He blusters out through the long, curtained windows, heading into the empty white room, a false smile plastered across his face as he moves through the door, shutting it behind him. Shutting it with me on the outside!

'Hey, Stella, Ezra.' His greeting is warm. Undaunted.

'Marco?' Stella's voice rises in delight. 'What are you…?'

'Absolute bummer, the secret balcony is out of order,' he says confidently.

'What?' Ezra sounds a little disbelieving.

'Yeah. Can you believe that?' Marco chimes in with all the ease of a professional liar. 'All closed off. Health and safety.'

'Oh,' Stella says, a touch of disappointment in her voice. 'Never mind. Have you heard the music in the Assembly Hall?'

I move shakily to my feet, and there's the ear-splitting sound of glass crunching. I look down. It's my phone. I just stood on my sodding mobile phone! Outside, the voices continue, oblivious.

'I haven't been there yet,' Marco says with genuine delight. Their voices fade into everyday chatter as they move out of the room. Chatter that I'm fully aware would never include me. Not in a million years. I'm not part of this world. Standing hidden behind the closed doors, I realise exactly what it is that I am – the dirty secret.

MARCO

I'm not entirely sure how we get from the public rooms to the small room upstairs. One minute we're downstairs drinking in this woman's voice. I mean, the singer in the Connaught Room has a beautiful voice, but, the next minute, I'm taking Clara onto the balcony over the secret garden. I know it's amazing. I know it has this kind of special charm about it. I've been going there since I was a kid, mainly to avoid my parents. But tonight, I just want to be a bit closer to Clara, and the balcony is small!

'Isn't it incredible?' I say with a proprietorial air, like I own the place.

She has both hands clamped over her mouth, and her eyes are wide with awe. I have to admit, it's prettier and more enchanting than I remember. The courtyard below is lit up by golden lights hidden in the wall, which cast glittering ripples across the water. It's like some piece of magic. There's the sound of the water, the trailing plants – jasmine and bougainvillea. The place is a knockout.

Then she leans forward over the balcony; stupidly, I do the same and my hand brushes hers. The feeling that shoots through my body is like nothing I've ever felt before. I pull away, but then she's pulling me back towards her. She has to feel it too – this attraction, this force between us. Soon she's yanking me down by my tie and gripping my hair as I hoist her up onto my body. I no longer care about our boss–employee relationship. I'm not interested in business. Hell, I don't even care about the missing songbird. All I want is Clara, with her silk-covered waist, her beautiful curves, and her hot mouth against mine. My hands roll across her body, loving every inch of it. I'm kissing her lips, her chin, her neck, as if I'm a drowning man and this is my only possibility for life, for air.

Once we're both satisfied and spent, I keep my arms locked around her, not wanting to give her up. Never wanting to let go of her, not for as long as I live.

'You okay?' I ask, brushing a strand of hair back behind her ear and nuzzling my chin against the top of her head. Nuzzling it hard, wanting to do it all, every moment, all over again. Suddenly, my heart stops. The breath in my lungs catch in my throat. Voices. There are voices outside. Someone is coming towards the balcony. The secret balcony. Someone is going to be breaking in any moment and finding us. I can't do that, not to Clara. I need to protect her.

Telling her to wait, I pat myself down and bluster out through the door, pushing it closed behind me. I have to keep Clara away from prying eyes.

'Hey, Stella, Ezra…' I call out brightly. 'Bit of a bummer. It's all closed off. Health and safety. Loose banister.' I steer them back towards the main door, leaving Clara safely behind us.

CHAPTER 14

CLARA

We are sitting in the dim interior light of the car, parked just outside the dark, cavernous cave of the hotel's underground garage.

'Do you want to talk about it?' Minty asks, looking in bewilderment at my phone with its cracked screen, no doubt wondering if he can fix it himself.

Cheeks streaked with tears, dress up around my knees in a scrunched mess, I'm no longer the fairy princess that I'd thought myself to be only hours earlier. I am dishevelled, abandoned, and feeling used and naïve. I just let some rich, entitled, over-privileged womaniser have his way with me in a public place. My cheeks burn with shame. It's not just my phone that's damaged goods. I had rung Minty from the balcony, the mobile had at least held together for that. I'd asked my brother if he could bring a car around to the back. He did.

'What happened?' he says, still scrutinising the pathetic phone with its dim, pleading lights emanating out through the damage.

'I stood on it,' I say glumly.

He shoots me a worried look. 'Nah, C. I didn't mean the phone. I mean the tears?'

'It was a disaster.'

He nods as if this is oh-so predictable. 'Music types. So, job's gone belly up, it's no strawberries in the fridge?'

Despite myself, I manage a small, sad smile, as I attempt to fight back the tears. 'Sorry.'

He clears his throat, an irritated look flashing over his features. 'But this guy, sis, he didn't hurt you, did he?' Minty peers at me in the mirror.

'No, nothing. Not really.' I grab a handful of hair and push it back up into the clip that once held it. I need to get a grip. 'I've just been a little bit foolish.' I sigh. 'That's it.' It wasn't entirely the truth, but my foolishness certainly has a good deal to do with the mess I've found myself in.

Minty shrugs. 'My middle name's "Foolish".'

'Well, that makes two of us. You'd have thought Mum and Dad would have been more inventive.'

He laughs. 'Yeah, all that arty-farty stuff and still couldn't sort us out a state-of-the-art middle name a piece.'

'Some parents,' I say with a smile.

'You said it. Hey, you want to stop for a full fry-up?'

I could do with getting the dress back to Nelly. I shan't be needing it again. But I can't face Marco's friends without backup. I love Nelly, but I know his loyalties will always be with his best mate, and I don't even want to talk about Marco. It all feels too raw. I need somewhere neutral.

'Brekky?' I say, muscling a little optimism into my voice. 'Oh, go on then.' I manage to text Nelly, avoiding the crack in my phone screen. I tell him we'll be at Jack's. It's by the meat market. They're open all night. He can bring my clothes and I'll give him back the frock. I don't want to have anything more to do with Marco and his entitled lifestyle.

'Oh dear,' Nelly says, flouncing into the café.

It's the early hours of the morning. Dark outside. The smell of bacon and eggs lay heavily in the air.

'Well, this is a first.' Nelly looks around him apprehensively, dragging one finger across a Formica table. The place is immaculate. It may be a greasy spoon, but Jack keeps his tables clean and a floor you could eat off.

'You, girl, have me popping up in all the most off-the-grid places. I've never had one of my gowns end up at a meat market before.' He glances around him and places one finger on his long nose as though deep in thought. 'It would make a wild place for a photoshoot,' he mutters.

'It was on the way home,' I say, still feeling miserable.

'You fancy a coffee, mate?' Minty says. He's standing at the counter.

Nelly's eyes narrow. 'With a tot of something spicy?'

Minty and Jack look blank.

Jack examines his stockpile of condiments. 'I could do you a spot of sriracha in the mug, but it's your funeral.'

'Hmm, thanks, but...' Nelly slides his backside onto the leather bench, whips out a flask. 'I always come prepared.' He turns his attention back to me. 'So what happened?'

I sink my head into my hands. 'It was a disaster.'

Nelly shrugs. 'I figured. Brought you these.' He slides a portfolio case onto the shiny red tabletop, flips it open and draws out his posh blue stationery. 'You tried. I tried. You get the sayonara written, I'll drop it off.'

'Sorted,' I say feebly.

'Sorted,' he confirms. 'And... did anyone ask you about the dress?'

I shake my head feebly, failing to tell him that some woman had asked me if it was the fashion to wear dresses hooked up into your garter belt. I had left in a hurry! 'No,' I say simply.

'Philistines,' he states, equally simply. 'Well, these are yours.'

He pulls my work clothes out from his bag. 'Sorry, darling.' Nelly ruffles my hair. 'The man's just not ready for love.'

'I wasn't…' I protest.

'Oh, but you so were. Shame.' Nelly sighs. 'It would have been a great match. Made in heaven. Marco just loves places like this. It's his kind of hot sauce if you like.'

'Coffee for you,' Minty says, sliding a mug across the table towards Nelly.

'Great.' Nelly twists the neck of his flask and adds a slug of whisky. 'Now you,' Nelly says, fixing me with his deep brown eyes. 'Get your clothes off.'

And surprisingly, although this is one of the most beautiful gowns I have ever worn, will most likely ever wear in my entire life, I can't wait to get the thing off.

❧

The next day, I can barely get out of bed let alone go to work. So, I feel a sense of satisfaction that my letter of resignation will be winding its way into the world without me.

'What can I do?' Minty asks, standing in the doorway to my room, wiping his hands on the apron I got him last Christmas.

'Nothing,' I say, throwing a pillow over the back of my head and burrowing into my mattress.

'I'll call the doctor,' he says.

I don't need a medic. All I really need is space in which I can feel foolish. 'Seriously, Minty, I'm fine.'

He comes into the room, tiptoeing across the carpet, and lays one hand over my forehead. 'You're not hot. Then again…' he pauses, mulling something over in his brain. 'I think it has to go in the ear. That's where you get the best readings.'

'Nobody is sticking a finger in my ear,' I say firmly. 'Anyway, that's taking a temperature with a thermometer, not with your hands.'

'Ah, right,' Minty says. 'I always thought that was a bit unhygienic.' He glances suspiciously at his own hands. 'Oh, and by the way, you've had phone calls.' Uninvited, Minty takes up a pew, sinking down at the edge of my bed.

Phone calls? I cringe. Could it be Marco? I don't want to talk to Marco. He's probably ringing to ask me where his stapler is. 'Was it work?' I ask, simply unable to not pick that wound. Even talking about him sets my whole body reeling.

'Work, yes, one of the calls.' Minty shoots his eyes up into his forehead as he attempts to remember all the details. 'A lady called Betsy. She said you've got to work a week's notice, and you're best on reception.'

Well, at least that's one blessing.

'She also said she wanted to talk to you.'

My heart sinks. She must have seen the footage. Most likely they all know it was me who left the door open. I'm not in the mood for a showdown.

'And the other call?' I ask, nervously.

'Evelyn.' Minty smiles. 'From the choir. She wanted to check if you'd be there tonight. Something about a solo?'

'Oh, I can't,' I say, pulling the eiderdown up around my face.

Minty looks confused. 'What did you do, sis?' he asks gently. 'You can tell me.'

But of course, that is absolutely not possible. I cannot tell my brother that I've had sex in what may have seemed a private grotto but is essentially a public space. A one-time rough and tumble with an arrogant shit of a music producer. No. That information would not go down well.

'Whatever it is,' Minty says kindly. 'You need to stop beating yourself up over it. Life goes on.'

He's right, of course.

'Okay,' I sigh. 'Choir tonight.'

'Great,' Minty says brightly, pulling himself back up from my bed. Clearly relieved – as far as he's concerned, I'm a job done. He can get back to his precious cars. 'I'll drive you over.'

MARCO

I feel bloody awful when I wake. The fragments of the night before come back to me like painful shards of a broken mirror, each piece seeming to taunt me. After I'd got rid of Fitz's parents, I searched everywhere for Clara. But just like Cinderella, the woman appeared to have vanished into thin air. There wasn't even a shoe left on the hotel's steps. Although a handbag with her ID in would have been a lot more helpful. I had no idea where she lived and couldn't get into the HR records until the morning. So I just ended up wandering the streets like a zombie. Eventually, I must have wound my way back home and tumbled into bed in the early hours.

I don't think I've ever felt so confused in my life. Okay, so it could be because of the lack of sleep, but somehow, I don't think so. This woman is turning my head upside down. I need to talk to her. I have a quick shower, dress, and then grab a taxi into work. Luckily, no one's around. Natalie's our HR person, but I have the key to her office and can bypass her login code with my own. I grab myself a coffee from the kitchen, then head straight for Natalie's office. It's locked, but again, my fob gets me in. I sit in front of her screen and fire it up. My life at the moment seems like a total mess. I meet a woman I actually like, then blow it all by moving too fast. It's eight in the morning. She'll be at her desk by nine, but I'm desperate to get word to her. The way last night ended was all wrong. I take a long, hard slug of the hot coffee. It seeps through my body, shaking my brain cells into action. I can do this. I can pull this around. Personal files fill the screen. Shit. I hadn't realised so many people worked here. There must be over two hundred. Suddenly, I'm feeling even more on the back foot. If I can't pull this around, find our missing songbird, keep the broadcasters and the press happy, it's not just Delagado Sounds that will go tits up. The other businesses in the Tower might not be directly related, but there's a crossover with a lot of them. In addition, we're sharing the same space, feeding off the same infrastructure. All these files contain details of lives that will be devastated if the company goes bankrupt and we have to close the doors.

I push back in my chair. This is too much pressure. How had I not realised that so many people were dependent on me? The feeling of responsibility is utterly overwhelming, and a wave of guilt washes over me. I can't fail them. I won't fail them. This isn't just about me, or even Clara, anymore – it's about everyone at Delagado Towers. I know it's odd. I know it is totally irrational, but I can't help feeling that if I get Clara back, I can somehow pull everything around and find our missing songbird. Get the company back on track. I take a deep breath and focus on the screen. Her file must be here somewhere. She'd transferred only yesterday from reception. It won't have filtered through to my department, but it should be here on the company screen. I start scrolling through the employee records. With every flick of the mouse, I feel an overwhelming sense of nausea. All these souls. I'm responsible for all of these people. Suddenly I see the right file. C. Thompson. Ridiculous. I don't even know her last name, but this must be her. She's still registered as working in reception. With a sense of elation, I open the file. Yes! It even has a photo of her. Clara Thompson. My Clara. I punch her telephone number into my phone.

'What the hell do you think you're doing?' comes an irritated voice.

I look up, that foolish grin still plastered across my face. Betsy's standing in the doorway, scolding.

'Bets,' I say, barely able to hide the excitement. 'I wanted to get Clara's home address.'

But Betsy is not looking happy. In fact, the woman feels like an ice-cold wind as she steps purposefully across the office and pulls the plug out of the back of the computer.

'What?' I'm dumbfounded.

Betsy narrows her hard, grey eyes, and when she speaks, there's not an ounce of friendship in her voice, or human understanding. 'I need a word with you. Now.'

❧

CLARA

Once again, the crypt smells of incense and candle wax, the familiar scent that usually comforts me. Not today.

My stomach churns as I walk through the heavy wooden door. The choir is already gathered, warming up their voices with scales and arpeggios.

Evelyn spots me and waves me over enthusiastically. 'Clara, come join us, we're just about to start.'

I force a smile and make my way to an empty spot in the front row. My heart's pounding in my chest so hard it's practically drowning out the sound of the choir.

How could I have been so stupid? Marco wanted his bit of fun. That whole secret courtyard crap. I bet he takes all his lady friends there. I'm so mad at myself I could spit.

Evelyn taps her conductor's baton, bringing the chatter to a halt. 'Shall we begin with "Amazing Grace"?'

The choir nods, sorts through their sheet music in preparation.

Evelyn looks at me expectantly. 'Right, the solo, Clara.'

My face burns and my knees go weak. I just don't have the

confidence anymore. It feels as though I'm wearing my skin inside out – everything is far too painful, too raw.

I clear my throat. 'Evelyn, I... I don't think I should sing the solo today.'

Evelyn frowns, glances between me and the choir. I know she's wondering how to handle this delicately in front of everyone. She knows my confidence isn't the best and has worked so hard to bring me on. She smiles sympathetically, turns her attention quickly back to the choir. 'Susan, would you do the honours?'

Understandably, Susan looks thrilled at the opportunity.

And as Susan's voice echoes out through the crypt, it seems as if my entire life is leaving me behind. But I don't even feel envious. All I feel is relief. My mind is occupied with self-loathing, which is a meaty mode of operation. There's no room for wondering if Susan's better than me. I don't care. If only I hadn't been so utterly daft. I never have sex with a man on a first date, and last night wasn't even a date! What an idiot I've been.

Once again, I try to focus on the melody, to lose myself in the familiar words of 'Amazing Grace'. But each note only reminds me of what I've lost. By the time we reach the chorus, and the entire choir is supposed to come in, tears blur my vision and I start to sob. Everyone is looking at me. I can't do this anymore and make a break for the door.

There's a small garden in the churchyard. It's supposed to be a place of reflection and peace. I throw myself down onto the wooden bench dedicated with a small plaque to a guy named Tony. He's just going to have to budge over, although I'm not sure I'm going to be good company. Today I may be doing the reflection, but I'm not so sure about the peace.

'Clara?' I hear Evelyn's voice behind me. She reaches out gently and touches my shoulder before sitting beside me. Her face is full of concern. 'Whatever it is, it can't be that bad.'

I choke back a sob. 'You don't understand, Evelyn. I've made such a mess of things. And now...' I gesture helplessly at the choir. '...I can't even sing solo here anymore, and I'd worked so hard to get there.'

'It's not important,' Evelyn says firmly. 'You have worked hard. This is not a problem. Everyone has setbacks. Next week, you'll be fine. The important thing is, even if you take a few steps back, it doesn't mean you're heading in that direction permanently. You'll get your confidence back and start moving forward again. I promise.'

I wipe my eyes with the edge of my sleeve. 'It's been tough at work. I've been an idiot, actually.'

'So.' Evelyn shrugs.

'I left a door open, the office got burgled.'

'Ah.' Her tone changes. 'Did they take anything valuable?'

'Guitars, and it threw the audition log into chaos.' I sigh, unsure how much to tell Evelyn.

'And?'

How is it that everyone knows when I'm trying to hide something? 'I recorded my own voice. Left it in the office. Marco Delagado, the head of the company, he heard the recording and now he's obsessed with finding the voice.'

Evelyn frowns. 'Your voice.'

I nod. 'But...' My shoulders rise in an expression of true hopelessness. '...I can't tell him it's me because–'

'Of the stuff that's been stolen.' Evelyn exhales a long, low breath. 'That is a mess.'

'Oh, it gets worse,' I say miserably. 'I slept with him too.'

Evelyn chews her top lip. 'Hmmm.'

'Exactly.' I feel like a hopeless and very silly child. 'What do I do now?'

She rubs her hands over her skirt, flicks her nails as if thinking. 'Probably own up to having left the door open, and, I mean, is this a relationship?'

'Marco,' I scoff. 'No. After I slept with him, he just walked off.'

'Bastard!'

I feel totally shocked. Evelyn is a churchgoing chorister. Bad language is not in her repertoire.

'You think?'

She nods back an affirmative.

'I'm just not sure…' I draw my words out, trying to give myself a little thinking time. 'I'm not sure how I can move on from this. My voice, the recording, the robbery… the casual sex, which I swear is just not my style.'

Can I get thrown out of the choir for casual sex? I'm not sure. God, I wish I'd left that bit out. 'Everything is a total mess,' I say. Hoping that maybe Evelyn will forget about the sex bit. Although she did call him a bastard, so I'm guessing not.

She places one hand on my shoulder and gives it a gentle rub. 'Not everything is a mess. You still have your talent and your passion. Your confidence will come back, I promise. It's just taken a hit. Naturally. You've had a seriously fucked-up week.'

I laugh. 'Evelyn! Are you allowed to swear?'

She shoots me a hard look. 'When it's strictly and unavoidably necessary, damn straight. Now…' She drops her hand to her lap. '…chin up – let's finish this hymn.'

CHAPTER 15

CLARA

'Hey.' Stan does a double-take, walking back out of his door and taking a full circle around in the spinning carousel. 'I thought you'd boosted yourself off into the stratosphere.'

'Down to earth with the proverbial bump,' I say, trying to make it sound light. Trying to make it feel like I'm not dying inside, because I'm back, standing behind the marble reception desk.

'So, it didn't work out then?' he says with a sympathetic downturn of his mouth.

'Actually, it worked out perfectly. Only I wanted to get paid less and have less responsibility because I love your witty banter.'

Stan shrugs in a smug way. 'Can't put a price on a talent like mine. Speaking of which...' He ambles over to the desk. '...did they find that missing songbird they were looking for?'

I feel a little back-footed, not sure how Stan knows about the missing recording.

'No,' I say because I'm positive they haven't found her. She's me. I'd know.

'I guess it's early days,' Stan says.

'Am I missing something?' I can't help feeling that unless Stan sits and watches the seventeenth floor's CCTV footage twenty-four hours a day, he seems a little too in the know.

'Are you missing something?' he asks cooly. 'Haven't you seen today's paper?'

'Stan,' I say, exasperated. 'No, I haven't. Spit it out.'

'There's a copy under your desk.' He shrugs as he wanders away. 'What would you do without me?'

'Die, Stan,' I say, eagerly opening the newspaper. 'I'd die of boredom and ignorance.'

He laughs. 'Yup, that's about the size of it.'

But I'm not listening anymore. I'm desperately scanning down the front page. Delagado Sounds is in the headlines, well, at least Betsy is. Marco's face is nowhere to be seen. But according to Betsy, the offices were burgled. They're looking for their song-bird. They want everyone to send demo tapes. This could be the hunt of the century. But what I don't understand is where Marco is in all this. The light on my switchboard begins to flicker. Taking off my clip-on earring, I pick up the receiver. 'Reception. Delagado Towers. How can I help you?'

My heart sinks. It's Betsy, and she wants to see me. Now.

'Sorry,' I say. I'm actually not sorry at all, but sorry always sounds good if you need to stall. 'It's just me on reception.'

'Stan can cover,' Betsy says before putting the phone down. I stare at Stan, not sure that he can, in fact, cover. I'm wondering if I can pull another sicky or possibly run out of the building. They know. They must know it was me who left the door open.

MARCO

I barely slept last night. Betsy's words kept circulating through my brain. No, circulating is wrong. They didn't have that kind of direction. My thoughts were running around like a hive of poked ants: chaotic, angry, and lost. She didn't tell me the full bad news. She just went on and on about data protection and how just because I had the keys to the HR office, it didn't mean I could go snooping around looking for 'the new girl's' details. I'm not quite clear why she keeps calling Clara 'the new girl'. It's clearly some Betsy hang-up. I wish I hadn't got into bed with her. Not Clara, Betsy. Bed as in business bed. In fact, I feel the heat searing up and out of my collar; I didn't get Clara anywhere near a bed. My God, it was good. Amazingly good. I've just got to find some way of talking to her. She felt it too, I could tell. Unless she's the best actress ever, which is unlikely. The woman is just a receptionist secretary type. Perfect. Perfect for me.

I take a deep breath, but my thoughts are still doing the ant thing. I need to find out what Betsy wants. That's what I'm in for this morning.

I grab a coffee from the shop next door. Black. I put a spoonful of sugar in. Something has to sweeten up my day. I'm guessing my partner found the CCTV footage. It was in my bin, after all. I should have taken better care of it. Dropped it in the Thames or put it in a firecracker. A microwave would have done the trick. But no. I'd taken the shortcut and dropped it in the wastepaper bin. Somebody must have been snooping. Sure, it's a problem. The tape clearly shows me going into the office and taking the guitars off the walls. I fast-forwarded through it till I found the right bit. It's obviously me. The funny thing is that the guitars are actually mine. Dad gave them to me when I was sixteen; only I have nothing in writing. I should have taken the damn things during daylight hours. Explained the situation and just pulled them off the walls. Nobody would have objected. Only now, it looks odd. It looks like I'm stealing them. Maybe planning to put in some kind of false insurance claim. I'm willing to bet that's exactly what it looks like to Betsy. So there'll be a ticking off. She'll slap my wrists. I'll say sorry. Everything will sink back to normal. I take another slurp of coffee. It's bitter. The acrid smell is providing that much-needed wake-up shot. I guess it's best to get this over with as soon as possible.

I've seen the morning papers. Betsy's offering ten grand for a tape of our missing songbird. Ten grand. It's a great publicity stunt. I mean, maybe, actually, this shitshow could all work out for the best. The lift doors slide open and I stop for a moment, not taking a step out because something isn't right. Betsy, Fitz, and Clara are all gathered in my office.

'Speak of the devil,' Betsy says. Even though she's partitioned off from me by a glass wall, I can feel her anger. Wow. That woman is mad about those guitars.

'Come in, Marco,' she says, which is ironic since it's my office. 'You know Clara.'

Of course I know Clara.

'Sure.' I smile at her. It's a professional courtesy smile. Totally unrepresentative of how I'm feeling. I'm having to bite down on my lip to stop myself from smiling. I'll grab her on the way out, take her down in my lift where it's private, where we can talk. Where we can… images of last night flood my brain. Her body pressed against mine. Her face tilted back in ecstasy, eyes closed.

'Marco?' Betsy's voice breaks through my thoughts.

'Yeah.' I snap back to the present.

'You know what this is about?' she asks, but I'm not sure it's a question.

'Sure, the guitars.'

'Guitars?' Fitz, Betsy, and Clara all stare at me like I'm a martian.

'The ones off the wall.' I indicate into the reception area.

'No,' Betsy draws out the word before bringing her attention to Fitz. 'Fitz, are you happy to be here?'

Fitz's features look tight, drawn. The happy-go-lucky girl that is so Fitz appears to have disappeared. 'I feel I have to be,' she says shortly.

Betsy nods. 'It's come to our notice,' she says, drawing in a deep breath, 'that you have, in the past, had women up here in the studio.'

They have to be joking.

Betsy's eyes narrow. 'You've brought women up here after hours and plied them with drink.'

Clara's gaze drops to the floor. It's clear she can barely stand to look at me.

'Is that right?' Betsy says.

I run my hands around my collar, attempting to loosen it. 'Maybe three times,' I say. 'Three in total. We'd…' I glance over towards Fitz. 'It was when we split up. That month. August, I think it was.'

Fitz raises one hand dismissively. I'm not sure what it means.

'And I did not ply them with drink,' I say, my voice rising defensively. 'They all came up because they wanted to.'

'So they were stone-cold sober?'

'No, but…' I shrug. 'I mean, I didn't do a breathalyser test. One was teetotal. Another only drank sparkling mineral water. I think it was me that was worse for wear, not them.' I run one hand through my hair, hating being put on the spot. But I have nothing to hide. 'Have you had complaints? I can give you their numbers.' I reach for my phone. 'You can call them up, ask them.'

'Marco, stop,' Fitz says, her expression tight and pinched. 'It kind of goes wider.'

I slump down on the edge of my desk. I seriously don't want to be here. I can understand why Betsy's grilling me. Maybe. And Fitz is a partner in the company too. And there's the ghost of an emotional connection. Okay, so we were on a break, but still. I'm guessing nobody wants to hear about interim affairs. But Clara? Clara is something new. Something fresh. Something glorious. I don't want her dragged into the mud. 'Does Clara have to stay?' I ask.

'The problem is, Marco.' The way Betsy says my name is hard-bitten and sour. The woman is a serious B.I.T.C.H. I feel my anger rising. 'The problem is that there was a complaint about last night.'

Aghast, I look at Clara. Oddly, she looks right back at me, equally aghast.

'Someone complained. An anonymous tip that you were behaving badly towards an employee. Badly as in lecherously.'

'What!' I shout.

'No.' Clara's on her feet.

Betsy shoots her attention towards Clara. 'So nothing happened?'

'I-I…' Clara stutters. She looks so scared. 'No,' she says flatly. 'Nothing.' She glances towards me, a look of pain and hurt in her eyes. 'Absolutely nothing. I wasn't feeling well, so I left.'

Betsy nods. 'But you can see the problem, Marco. You've been inviting women up to the studio after lights out. Let me ask you this once and ask you this straight.' Her eyes burn like flint.

'I seriously wish you would.'

'Marco.' Fitz shakes her head. 'Anger is not going to get you anywhere.'

'For Christ's sake,' I say, so irritated I could throw something. Wishing I had a little office stationery to hand. 'What are you going to ask?'

Betsy clears her throat. 'Have you been auditioning young women after hours? Recording them and promising them record deals in return for…' she hesitates, '…favours.'

'Sex!' Fitz shouts angrily. 'What Betsy means is sex.'

'No!' I can't believe this is happening.

'So our missing songbird, how do you explain that?' Betsy says. Shifting her weight slightly in her court shoes, getting ready for the kill. There's no way she's backing down.

'I have no idea.' I drag both hands across my face. Confused, defensive, hurt.

'Nobody remembers the mystery woman, Marco,' Fitz says

sadly. Her whole body looks crushed. 'Terry and Jeff, Clara. I even rang Amy and played her the tape. Nothing.' She shoots me a pained look. There are tears in her eyes.

I can't believe how stupid I've been. I end up crushing everything I've ever loved, just like my father.

'You can see the problem,' Betsy says, her voice sounding terse.

I'm not sure I can. What I can see is that Clara has large tears forming in those beautiful blue eyes.

'I'm going to have to ask you to take a leave of absence. We can't have you in the office,' Betsy says, shaking her head in what might, if you didn't know her well, be considered as a sad attitude.

Clara staggers to her feet. 'I'm sorry, I don't feel well.' She's crying. 'Please believe me, though.' She looks down at her feet. 'Mr Delagado didn't take advantage of me.' Her voice cracks. 'I'd like that on record.'

Betsy nods. 'I'll see you to the lift.'

Clara smiles a thin, sad smile.

'I don't believe any of this,' I say, starting to pace. Wanting to run after Clara, but no doubt, if I did, Betsy would have me for harassment. What a mess if I take even one step after her.

'Oh, Marco.' Fitz sighs.

'Fitz, I swear there was nothing…'

'Hey.' She raises both hands to stop me. 'It doesn't matter. Have you ever wondered why we're not having sex anymore?'

I stop pacing. 'Sorry?'

'Our relationship. It's not physical. You must have noticed.'

'Well.' I shrug. 'Yeah, I mean, I think it's more friendship.'

'Brotherly,' Fitz says, wrinkling her nose. 'I'm in love with Terry.'

'What?' My jaw practically hits the floor. 'Keyboard Terry? The musician?'

'His last name is Mitchel, but yeah. And he normally plays a piano, but yeah, that's the one.'

'Sorry?' Confused, I slump in my chair.

'Yes. I'm totally and utterly in love and obsessed with the guy. He feels the same way, only…' She shrugs. 'You know what my dad's like.'

I know exactly what her dad's like. Terry would never be good enough.

'So.' She smiles sadly. 'You were convenient.'

'And… you bought into the company? Why do that?'

'Because you've run it into the ground. If Terry's out of a job, it'll mean he gets embarrassed. The difference between what I have, which is a…' She waves her arms in a wide circle. 'It's a lot. And what he has – musician's union rates. Well, there's a sizeable gap. I can't give him money. He's too proud, but I can make sure his job's secure. That's all I'm doing. But you…' She stands, reaches for her bag and straightens her short tan mini-skirt. 'You, Marco, need to get your shit together.'

❧

CLARA

I don't want to be here. I'm not sure why Betsy's taken over Marco's office, or why Fitz and Betsy keep giving me sympathetic looks, but none of it's making me comfortable.

'I feel, it's more…' I hesitate. 'Stressful on the seventeenth floor than it is in reception,' I say. They haven't asked me, but this has to be about my letter of resignation.

'And.' Betsy fixes me with her hard eyes. 'Is there anyone in particular who has made the experience stressful for you?'

I want to say, yes, you. But I'm not sure that would go down well. Besides, I'm absolutely and utterly convinced that is not what she's fishing for.

'To be honest, I think I'm happier on the reception desk,' I say. 'Besides, it's–' I hear the lift open. When I look up, I see Marco striding towards the office, looking as confused as I feel. I reach for my bag. 'I think maybe I should–'

'Sit,' Betsy says firmly, and I don't dare to disobey.

What follows is possibly the worst fifteen minutes of my life. Betsy starts grilling Marco. I mean, seriously grilling him. At first, I can't work out what the agenda is. It sounds like complaints of sexual harassment. I feel my chest tighten. Am I just the latest in a score of women he's been having sex with alfresco? Is that his thing? In the office, out at the Beaumont. I am so naïve. But Marco insists it's not true. He was having a break from Fitz. He'd met a few women, just a few. They were all consenting. He even offered to give Betsy their numbers so she could check it out. Only then does Betsy drop her bombshell. She accuses him of offering 'private' auditions. The kind where he brings girls up to the studio and records their voices in return for sexual favours. The only evidence Betsy has, the only evidence for all of that, is the missing songbird. I manage to get to my feet. My head is swimming, and I feel sure any minute I'm going to crash to the floor or scream. I need to get out, but before I go, I need to do the decent thing. I wasn't drunk last night. He didn't coerce me into anything. I wanted him, genuinely wanted him. Even now, here, with all the walls of normality crashing down on him, I still want him. Maybe he used me, but I used him too.

'I'm sorry.' Tears sting my eyes. 'I don't feel well…' I can't look into his eyes. Can't look at the man any longer. I have to leave. 'Mr Delagado didn't take advantage of me.' My voice cracks. 'I'd like that on record, please.'

Betsy nods, although I can't help thinking she looks disappointed.

'I'll see you to the lift.' Her words sound curt and businesslike. Ever the professional.

And that's it. The end of a love story. The end, before it even had a chance to fly.

CHAPTER 16

CLARA

Everything about Evelyn's house is lovely. It's not big, but it's homely. It's not swish, but it's comfortable. There are finger paintings on the fridge and a large bowl with fruit, apples, pears, and grapes resting on the generous surface of the long wooden table.

'I didn't know where else to go,' I say miserably, staring into the china teacup Evelyn's pushed in front of me.

She's jiggling Thea, her eighteen-month-old on her hip. I can't believe that a house can be so organised when there's this little bundle of chaos in its midst.

'You did exactly the right thing,' Evelyn says, popping Thea into her highchair and squeezing those chubby legs through the leg holes. 'So, tell me all about it.' Evelyn plonks herself down in the carver's chair opposite me. 'All the gory details.'

'Sordid, Evelyn,' I correct.

'That bad?' Her face furrows into a concerned frown.

'Oh,' I sigh. 'It's so much worse.'

My worries seem so different from anything Evelyn could conceive. This is a home. This is a family. My own family circumstances are such a bunfight in comparison. The smells of the evening meal waft over me. Everything here is perfect; in contrast, I am such a mess. Tears prick my eyes as I relay the whole sorry story, ending it all with a plea to the universe. Well, okay, a plea to Evelyn.

'I can't believe Marco's been fired. It's his business. Can Betsy do that?'

Evelyn shrugs. 'As soon as he took stakeholders on, it all becomes way more complicated.'

'But if I hadn't left the door open. If the files hadn't gone missing, none of this would have happened.'

'Okay. Stop, right there,' Evelyn says, rapping on the table as though summoning me to silence. 'You can't keep blaming yourself. Marco was drunk and angry and sacked his PA. You jumped in at the last minute and pulled everything into shape.'

I drop my head onto the table. 'I lost all the auditions. Two weeks' worth.'

'No.' Evelyn reaches across the table and grabs my hand. 'You didn't lose the auditions. You lost the ones you were logging, but only in the format Betsy wanted them in. Everything else is still there. The problem was they didn't recognise the voice.'

'Because I didn't sing for them.'

'So, it's simple, isn't it?'

Thea chuckles.

'Oh, don't mind her.' Evelyn smiles. 'She thinks life is easy-peasy. Give her a biscuit and she's happy. It sounds like Betsy's at the root of this web.'

'She's convinced he's been seducing every woman that comes into the office, but it's not true.'

Evelyn tuts, edging her chair next to me and patting my knee. 'Maybe she's not exactly convinced. Maybe it just suits her.' Evelyn squeezes my hand, her blue eyes soft with sympathy. 'I understand how frightening it can be to put yourself out there. Honestly, I do. I used to get terrible nerves.'

'Seriously?' Somehow, it's hard to imagine the cool, calm, and collected Evelyn as ever being nervous.

'Sure. It's part of being human. It doesn't mean you shouldn't push yourself. Besides, you can't let Marco take the blame for this. It's totally wrong. So it's time to embrace your talent – show everyone who the real songbird is. Prove to Betsy that Marco wasn't abusing his position. Clear his name.'

I feel myself breaking out in a cold sweat at the thought of it. 'But what if I'm not good enough?' The memory of the choir rehearsal yesterday still stings – I couldn't even sing with them, so how am I supposed to sing solo in front of a whole studio?

Evelyn gives me an encouraging smile, as if reading my thoughts. 'You have a gift, Clara. You just need to believe in yourself. Now, drink up. We have planning to do! I'll help. Rehearsal every night till we nail it.'

I grin, raise my teacup. Maybe Evelyn's right. Maybe this is my chance to finally step into the spotlight. Besides, Marco might not have treated me well, but there's just something about him. I can't get him out of my thoughts.

'Do you think it's stupid to fall for a bad guy?' He might not have seduced women in his office, but there was no denying he had that crazy rock star thing going on.

'My advice?' Evelyn gave me a long, hard stare. 'Don't go judging till you know all the facts. Now, who else in that office has a vested interest in the company?'

There's only one person who springs to mind – Fitz. But would she even want to talk to me?

❧

'Are you collecting?' An immaculate woman in her sixties, with glossed red hair bouffanted in a stylist-dried bob stares at me over fashionable, thin-framed glasses before giving Evelyn and

Thea a disapproving once over. I might even have detected a shiver when she ran her eyes over the baby.

'Collecting? No,' I say, taken aback. Not sure what I would be collecting for. But I am instantly feeling like someone from a different, more inferior race.

'I work for your daughter.'

Stella Fitzwilliam looks puzzled.

'At Delagado Towers,' I say, wondering how this is going to work.

I've had to bring Evelyn with me because I need backing, not the musical kind, the backing-up-the-truth kind, and possibly the emotional kind. And Evelyn had to bring baby Thea with her because, apparently, that's the deal with babies – if you're going somewhere, so are they. 'Is Fitz in?' I say, a wobble of uncertainty in my voice. Already I'm filled with an overwhelming desire to take off at a fast sprint in the other direction.

Stella glances back over her shoulder into the massive marble hallway of the Fitzwilliam home. A magical fairy tale of a place with white stuccoed columns, large Georgian sash windows, and multiple sills covered in barges of window boxes that spill colourful plants. Sweet-scented pink geraniums. A brilliance of blue lobelia, some shouty purple trumpets of trailing petunias, and even some dwarfed dahlias with dark stems and crimson flowers. It is an absolute enchanted storybook of a place.

Stella stands back from the doorway and shouts up into the empty house. 'Darling?' Her voice echoes around the hall, which is tiled with a checkerboard floor and has a vast ceiling. 'Visitors.' She turns back towards us. 'You better come in.' She takes a step back. Evelyn and I follow her into the hallway. Every alcove and sideboard in the house is laden with vases of flowers. The most beautiful arrangements imaginable.

'Wow. These are incredible.' I reach out to touch the soft petals of a sunburnt orange lily.

'I have a man,' Stella tells us dismissively. 'You can wait in here. My daughter always takes a while to muster herself.' She pushes open the door to a grand drawing room. Plush sofas in brilliant blues and pale yellows, their cushions perfectly plumped, await us. The entire place smells like a hotel. A vanilla bean hotel. I have to fight the urge to inhale loudly. 'I'd offer you refreshments, but it's the housemaid's morning off. We have to do it now, legally. People need time off.' She laughs as if the thought is ridiculous. 'It's very inconvenient. I still haven't mastered the kettle.' Stella sighs as if this is totally beyond her. 'My daughter will be down soon. I'd appreciate it if you didn't let the baby…' she waggles one of her braceleted arms, '…excrete any body fluids.'

'Never,' Evelyn replies in total seriousness. A seriousness that gives Stella cause to double-take.

There's a tense moment before Stella nods dismissively and exits through the door. 'Work?' she mumbles under her breath with a bemused curiosity.

'What was that?' Evelyn hisses in her wake.

'Fitz's mum.'

For some reason, Thea chooses that exact moment to let loose a delightful peal of giggles. I'm so glad I brought them both. People like Evelyn keep me grounded.

'Oh?' Fitz says, pushing open the door and finding us there. I get the feeling we were not what she was expecting. She's wearing a cut off Iron Maiden T-shirt, her arms and throat are circled with bling, and her skirt looks like black PVC, but I'm guessing it has to be leather.

'Sorry to bother you at home,' I jump straight in. 'I just, I…' Evelyn is standing behind me and gently places her hand on my back. I have to do this. 'It's… I have some important information, and I didn't know who else to turn to.'

For an excruciating moment, Fitz just stands there eyeing us, and I seriously think this has all been a total waste of time. Then suddenly, she nods a brief acknowledgement.

'Okay,' she says. 'You better come downstairs. This place…' She glances around her. 'It's like a museum.'

One of the great things about Fitz is that she knows how to operate a kettle and amuse a child. Within five minutes, we're all gathered around the kitchen table in the basement. All the adults have mugs of tea, and Thea has been given an assortment of spoons to play with.

'I'm sorry,' Fitz says, drawing a hand through her purposefully straggly up-do of dark hair. 'I probably should have spoken to you yesterday after the meeting, but I needed to…' She takes a deep breath. 'I needed to talk to Marco. Get things straight.' She pulls back a chair for herself and takes a seat at the table, idly playing with Thea's new collection of spoons. 'You needed to talk?' She doesn't look at us.

'Yes,' I say, glancing awkwardly at the cuticles on my nails, wishing I didn't have to do this. Evelyn gives me a small, gentle nudge. 'Marco wasn't inviting women up to the studio to sing.'

'I know.' Fitz sighs, dipping one of the spoons into her mug and giving it a stir, before extracting the metal and sticking it in her mouth like a lollipop. 'But it's impossible to prove. We all own a third of the shares. Betsy wanted to buy more from me two days ago. Thankfully, I said no. She thinks I haven't realised we're sitting on a collapsing gold mine. I don't quite know what her angle is.' Fitz narrows her eyes. 'But clearly, she wants to be a majority stakeholder and to get Marco out.'

'So she wants the business, even though it's not profitable?' Evelyn asks.

Fitz nods. 'No doubt she's got some merger deal up her sleeve. But this…' Fitz leans back in her seat, turning both palms upwards on the table in dismay. 'The lost tape, the stolen guitars, the selling promises to young starry-eyed hopefuls in return for–' She shivers. 'I mean, seriously. I know Marco. He may have lots of faults.' She glances up towards the ceiling, rapping her fingers on the table. 'He does have lots of faults, but using women like that.'

I feel my throat tightening. 'You're involved with him.' There's a weight of sadness that settles on my shoulders at the admission. Then Fitz does the oddest thing. She stands, goes to the kitchen door, and closes it gently.

'It's unlikely that my mother would venture this far into the bowels of the house.' Fitz raises an eyebrow ironically. 'But better safe than sorry.' She steps back towards the table. 'Involved?' She muses over my words. 'Involved with Marco.' She eases herself back into her chair, clasping her hands on the table in front of her. 'I love Marco, absolutely and utterly.'

My heart sinks. Of course she does. This is Marco's world. Fitz and Marco are the kind of marriage crafted in heaven. The ones that you see splashed all over the glossy magazines or in the papers.

'I love Marco,' Fitz continues, 'as a brother.'

Even though Marco and I are a total and absolute impossibility, I feel a rush of emotion, excitement, and elation wash over me. 'Honestly?' I gasp.

She shrugs. 'It's my parents. Marco is suitable material, cut from the right cloth.' She wrinkles her nose. 'They're terrible snobs.' She shoots me a sad look. 'They can't help it. Public schools and only mixing with posh friends can narrow a person's horizons.' She draws in her cheeks as though finding the whole topic distasteful. 'They've kind of been emotionally stunted, and it's too difficult to fight it now. Lost generation and all that. So I just pretend I'm in love with Marco. Besides…' She shoots me a serious look. 'I don't believe he'd take women up to the studio and exploit them. It's just not Marco's way.'

I blush, remembering the night of passion on the balcony. Was he exploiting me then? I'm not sure. He wasn't promising me anything. To Marco, I was just a receptionist. One that didn't have any dreams of stardom.

'But it's so tricky.' Fitz pushes one elbow onto the table, rubs her temples with her French-manicured nails. 'There's this missing woman. Was there something going on there? Some kind of promise? Betsy's offering a reward to find her, but half of me gets the feeling she doesn't really want to find the voice. She just wants a flood of other possibilities. To Betsy, the possible sexual harassment is useful. If we could just find that missing voice, we could clear his name.'

I feel Evelyn's eyes burning into me and clear my throat. 'I think I can help with that,' I say. 'It's me.'

Fitz's reaction is the most glorious ever. Her eyes light up, her pink lips drop open in excitement, and she claps her slim hands gleefully. I feel like the best Christmas present ever.

'Amazing! Amazing! Amazing!' Fitz calls out, delighted.

MARCO

It's two in the afternoon. I'm still in my boxers and the white vest I wear to sleep in. I haven't showered or changed. Below me lies the city. All those people rushing to their jobs. Everyone thinks they have somewhere to be, something important and urgent to do. In truth, it's all a lie. A fabrication to keep mankind on the treadmill.

My flat is large. The penthouse apartment of a block. The floor-to-ceiling windows give me Thames views on one side and the Limehouse Marina on the other. I know it's daft, but I love the canal boats; so small but so perfect. People chugging in, chugging out, getting on with their lives. Look the other way, and I see that snake of a river, old Father Thames, flood in and flood back out again, relentless. Seeming to say each morning, 'Still here?' Waiting for the day when I'm not. Sometimes I hate that river. It's got the same rush attitude that the entire city lives by.

I've got the compulsory large terrace, complete with hedging and lounge-like furniture. Hedging, even though I'm fifteen floors up. I have more garden than most of the terraced houses lying to the east of my glass-and-steel building. I'm a fan of glass and steel. My dad liked glass and steel. Am I like him? I cringe with embarrassment when I think of Clara. When I think of what I did to her. I took advantage. I shouldn't have done it. She was all buoyed up on the glamour of the evening, and I literally backed her up against a wall. But the thought of those lips on mine, of the way she pulled me down by my tie, clawed at my body with her nails. Letting out a long, low groan.

I kick the kitchen units. It hurts. They're expensive. Hobbling back to the bar stools that are set around my gleaming marble island, I nurse my throbbing foot, feeling like a total idiot. In fact, I am a total idiot. Not even Fitz is actually in love with me. She's just using me because I'm a convenient cover. I'm not totally convinced I know how I feel about that. I groan again. This time there's no physical pain, just an exhaustion at being me, as I flop my entire upper body across the cool marble. Everything is lost.

If only I could talk to Clara. Explain. If only I could tell her I truly found her totally confusing. The most exciting, magnetising, incredible person I have ever met in my life. If I could just ask her if she felt the same way. That's all. That's all I want. Just one meeting to set all this straight. Sod the job. Sod the business. Sod the accusations and the stolen guitars. I just need Clara. Then it dawns on me, one of the doormen. She had been talking to one of the doormen at the Beaumont. It seemed like she knew him. He had been touching her. An ex-boyfriend? Possibly. It might not go well if I start asking an ex-boyfriend questions. Then again, if I tell him it's for a job – that I have something for her. He looked like the hard-up type. If I can make it in his interests, maybe I can get to see her again. Only, I have to be careful.

This could all backfire. It could. But for the first time in twenty-four hours, I'm feeling alive. That dog of depression, of self-loathing, has lifted. To get to Clara, I need to find that mystery man. Luckily, they know me at the Beaumont. I can make up some story – I need valet parking for an event. A smile spreads across my face as I stare down at the city. My city. My town. And somewhere out there, is my girl.

CHAPTER 17

CLARA

The last place in the world I want to be is sitting on the low, louche red sofas of Delagado Sounds. To add insult to injury, I see they've replaced me. A slip of a girl with long blonde hair tied in a ponytail that she keeps swishing. She's clearly obsessed with her nails. Which are pretty, but they are going to present a problem when typing, phoning, filing, and just about anything else that comes under the remit of her job description. I wonder why Betsy didn't go back to Amy. Amy at least knew the job inside out. Then again, maybe that was Betsy's plan; she was cleaning out the old and making way for the new – Betsy's brand of new.

My one consolation about being back here is that this time, I'm not alone. I may have dropped Evelyn back home, but I have a different kind of secret weapon now – Fitz, and she's on my side. Fitz doesn't have to sit on the red leather sofas, seeing as she kind of owns the place. She's with Betsy. I can see them through the glass panels of Marco's office, which Betsy appears to have re-appropriated. Their mouths are opening and shutting, but there's no sound coming out. I wish I could lip-read. Luckily, I won't have to. Fitz turns towards me and mouths, 'In.'

I smile sweetly at the girl with the ponytail as I pass by. As I pull open the glass door to the office, I feel a hardcore gut wrench of fear. I'm guessing Betsy's going to ask me to sing. I will need to prove myself. At Fitz's, Evelyn had backed me up. She'd heard the tape and could categorically confirm it was my voice that was on it, warbling away. But Fitz hasn't really heard my voice, just a scattering of notes. I'm guessing Betsy's going to want the full deal.

'Close the door behind you and take a seat,' Betsy says, barely looking up from (what has clearly become) her new desk. It's scattered with audition tapes and files. I heard through the papers that Delagado Sounds is receiving two hundred files a day. Two hundred people claiming to be the missing songbird. It's proving to be great publicity.

'So.' Betsy flops herself into her cushioned desk chair. Places her elbows on the table, clasps her hands, and leans forward so she can fire an eye glare at me. 'You worked in the lobby then you were a PA for a matter of days.' She raises one sceptical eyebrow. 'And now you claim to be our missing songbird.'

I find my body tensing, which is difficult because the couch in Marco's old office is low and like liquid jelly. I wish I weren't so low. I feel as though I have no control. As though I'm a child, and that flippant rendition of all my recent past jobs makes me sound like a climber at best and a full-on flake master at worst. 'That's right,' I say. 'It's my voice on the tape.'

Betsy takes a long breath in, pauses to scratch her chin for a moment. 'So you came up here and recorded it?'

'Yes.'

Her eyes narrow. 'You'd only been working here for a nanosecond. How did you even get in? Marco?' There's a hard, caustic joy in her tone when she says his name.

'No.' I shake my head, trying desperately to adjust my flailing buttocks on the soft couch. 'It was that first day. You wanted me to re-log everything in your format.'

'The file that got lost.' Her lips harden into a thin line.

'Yes, but I did it.' I glance awkwardly down at my hands. 'There was a lot to do. I went out for supper.' I don't want to tell Betsy about my disastrous date with Robin. 'And then came back to finish it off.'

'What time?'

'Sorry?' This is beginning to feel uncomfortably like an interrogation.

'What time did you finish?'

'Oh, about one in the morning. I put it in your in-tray.'

There's an awkward pause.

'You're asking us to believe that you recorded it all by yourself?'

I shrug. 'It's not so difficult. I'd been helping all day.'

'And then the office is burgled.'

I cringe. Did I leave the door open? I must have done. 'I realise it doesn't look good. That perhaps someone was waiting outside and got in after I left. I guess you must have it all on the CCTV footage.'

Betsy pushes back in her chair. 'It's lost.'

'Lost?' Fitz sounds incredulous.

'Well.' Betsy moves around to the front of the desk, leans back against it, giving her even more height. 'The tape was handed to Marco, and that was the last anyone saw of it.'

Oh dear. This just seems to get worse.

'And you're sure Marco wasn't in here with you recording the track?'

'No.' I shake my head emphatically. 'It was just me.'

She begins to pace the office; Fitz and I glance at each other. I'm not convinced this is going well. There's an utter, overwhelming sense of relief when Betsy the dragon woman comes to a halt and folds her arms in a gesture of finality before firing off deductive analysis detective style.

'Well, the burglary and the missing songbird could be two

separate things. So, let's look at your claim first. You say the missing voice is yours.'

I nod.

'I heard her do some scales,' Fitz says. 'It's the same.'

Betsy shoots Fitz an irritated glance. 'Scales?'

Fitz shrugs. 'A bit of scat singing, and she had a friend there.'

I'm not comfortable with them calling me 'she'. It makes me feel like some subspecies, but I get the feeling I'm in no position to protest.

'Her friend was actually Clara's choirmaster.'

'Choir?' Betsy is looking totally bewildered.

Fitz sighs. 'Clara sings with a choir.'

Betsy turns her attention back to me. I squirm slightly.

'It's her,' Fitz says casually. 'And she's said without a doubt there was no coercion or promises of favours. Marco wasn't even in. Clara did it all by herself.'

Betsy swings the back of her chair around so the seat's open and ready for her and lowers herself onto it.

'Okay, suppose what you are saying is true.' Fitz flicks all the files and demo tapes piled high on Betsy's desk. 'It'll stop this headache.'

Betsy nods. 'It's certainly one problem solved. Okay. Let's make it Thursday. You come into the studio and record something. The same number on the tape and one other.' She shrugs. 'You know the tape. It would be easy enough to impersonate it. If the tape is you, you get the contract, but…' She slices the air between us with her hard eyes. '…not the reward money. This entire mess.' Betsy waves her hands across the piles of submissions on her desk. 'This was all unnecessary.'

That seems reasonable enough. 'Okay,' I say. I should be able to do it. I know Terry and Jeff. They like me. They'll support me. It's not as if I'll be singing solo in public for an audience.

Fitz gets to her feet. I have a feeling this meeting is over. 'You'll drop the harassment charges against Marco?'

'If this girl is our missing songbird.' Betsy eyes me critically. 'Nobody else has come forward.'

I get the nasty feeling she's been pushing people to testify against him. Poor Marco. This really is a witch hunt.

'So yes.' Betsy sighs. 'Yes, those charges will automatically be dropped. But she...' Betsy shoots me one of her hard dragon looks yet again. '...she is going to need to prove to us beyond doubt that she's the one we're looking for.'

❧

MARCO

The red carpet is gone. The stone steps look exposed and hard. There's no valet parking today, only the doorman dressed in white livery and gloves, standing beside the door with an instant smile on his face.

'Mr Delagado,' he says, standing and pulling the thick glass panel back so I can walk through. The Beaumont looks very different now all the party people and the media show has vacated. The lobby sofas are back, and there are flower arrangements dripping over tables and sideboards. There's a guy playing a baby grand in a corner. Tinkering away, filling the air with ambient sound.

'Can I help you, sir?' an androgynous woman says as she steps out from behind a low, teak reception desk. Like everything else at the Beaumont, the woman is immaculate.

'I...' I hesitate, not sure how I'm going to explain all of this. I certainly can't say I'm looking for a woman. That wouldn't go down well, and my half-baked idea about playing the rich card – looking for valet parkers – just seems all-out daft now. I should have thought about this more. My brain is spinning, grasping for plausible storylines as the woman with the slicked back hair and perfect red lips places her head gently to one side. Waiting.

Then, bingo I've got it – the perfect line.

'At the gala, I gave one of the valets my jacket to look after.' The excuse sounds okay, but will it fly?

She looks confused. 'You didn't put it in the cloakroom?'

'Cloakroom?' Of course, why wouldn't I put it in the cloakroom, but now I'm in the swing, it only takes me a beat to muster up an excuse. 'There was a queue. I was in a hurry. The valet said he'd take it. He was, I'm guessing, five ten. Fair-ish curly hair. Stubbled chin.' I'm slightly staggered at how easy I find it to recall so many details. I don't normally pay much attention to anything. But now, in this instance, there appears to be no end to my observational prowess. 'He was kind of–'

'Sorry, sir.' The woman holds up one hand. 'Just stopping you there. We have a lot of casual staff working at the Beaumont. However.' Her eyes glow with assured satisfaction. 'They are all excellent and very reliable. If he said he would drop it in the cloakroom for you, then it'll be there. I'll ask housekeeping.' She picks up the phone on her desk. 'Could you give me a description?'

Seeing as I appear to be so hot at doling out descriptions, I'm about to rattle off the details of my smartest blue overcoat when I realise, I'm wearing it! This storytelling business can wind a person in one hell of a fix.

After spending an hour trying to locate a jacket that doesn't exist, I give up. I don't want to leave my name and number 'in case it turns up' as I know for sure it won't. But helpful housekeeping insists. I leave the building with the curious feeling it's not just the imaginary coat that's lost; it's me. This is a big city. Would Clara be going back into the Towers? But I can't sit outside all day hoping I catch a glimpse of her. Besides, even if she does go into work, if Betsy catches me anywhere within snooping distance of the office, I feel pretty damn sure she'll call the police. I haven't done anything wrong. Not really. I shouldn't have come on to Clara. That was bad form. Even if she did reciprocate. I just want to do the decent thing. Say sorry. Hear her voice. Talk to her. Talk to her just once. Once and I'll be happy.

I decide to try the garage. The garage at the Beaumont is underground. The parking attendant might be wearing a suit, but he's much more amenable. Unfortunately, all the names of part-time staff are kept on the computer. You need a supervisor's key to unlock details. I slip him three hundred quid, and he assures me he can get me info on the mystery valet. It just might take time. As I walk away, I know this waiting around for someone to help tie up the missing dots and dashes as to who the guy is, has to be my last resort. Time seems achingly long. Pulled out and twisted into shapes I didn't even know it was capable of holding. Elongated beyond all recognition without work or Clara to fill in the hours and make them sing.

Wandering back down the road, I realise I have nowhere to go. I could go home to my fish tank apartment. I could look down on the city from my terrace. Watch the world going on below me; all those people sitting in their gardens, planting tomatoes, blowing up paddling pools, while all the time my large plush terrace stands empty and alone, with just Johnny-no-mates to look out over the view, mocking me. No. I don't want to do that. Then it hits me – Nelly. I'll go talk to Nelly. Maybe he knows where Clara lives.

'I can't believe you let that one go.' Nelly is up to his arms in dressing a woman. 'Breathe in just one more tiny…'

The woman does as instructed, pulling air into her cheeks as Nelly fastens some kind of cord. The woman with the dark hair and photoshoot look smiles as she drops her skirts around her legs. 'That should hold,' she says, patting her hips.

'Take fifteen, honey,' Nelly says. 'Just don't eat, drink, or laugh.'

The woman nods before walking stiffly off towards God knows what possible pursuits have been left open to her.

'Now.' Nelly turns his attention back to my sorry face. 'Clara. What did you do to piss that lovely young woman off so badly?'

'Sorry?' I have no idea where this is going.

'At the gala.' Nelly waves his hand as if these details are oh-so-pedestrian and boring. 'She described the event as…' He pauses. 'Okay, these are her words, not mine.'

I nod, eager to hear anything she had to say.

'A disaster,' he says simply, with a finality I'm not keen on.

'Disaster?' I say, confused. 'What exactly did she mean by *disaster?*'

'Her words.' Nelly shrugs. 'I'd say disaster is one down on the enjoyment scale from total fuck-up and one up from Armageddon. So,' he purses his lips, 'well done, you.'

'Not funny.'

In sympathy with Nelly's garage-style leather couch, I sink deeper into my shoulders. I'm feeling so grouchy. If there was a bin, I'd climb right in.

'She was lovely. Gorgeous. Sweet,' Nelly says, plucking at the air with his hands as he delivers each adjective, just to lay the cuts that bit deeper.

'Nelly, stop,' I groan, placing my hands against my ears. 'I feel like a total fuck-up. And they've kicked me out of the Towers.'

Nelly looks shocked. 'You're joking, right?'

I shake my head.

He grabs a seat with casters and scoots up to me; suddenly, the playfulness has vanished.

'This missing voice,' I say, feeling irritated, feeling as if I've gone through this so many times. Although, having said that,

Betsy has given the narrative a whole new twist. 'Betsy says that I coerced someone. Promised them a recording deal in return for…'

'A shag?' Nelly offers helpfully.

'Yeah,' I say.

'Shit.' Nelly's permanent joy and animation seem to have slid. 'But…' His eyes narrow. 'Not Clara? This has got nothing to do with Clara?'

'Absolutely nothing.'

'No.' He looks thoughtful as he eases the cuticles down on his thin fingernails, mulling the whole thing over. 'Cos, it's clear she's into you and that you're into her.'

'I'm not–'

Nelly throws his hands up in despair. 'Best friend here. I know you…' He waves one wand-like finger in front of my face in a circular motion. 'Know you inside out and upside down. You are *so* into her.'

I'm feeling all the tells of a desperate man, and actually seriously not giving a fuck anymore.

My phone vibrates in my pocket, and for one bliss-infused moment I think it'll be her. Even though she's never called me, and I'm not even sure she's got my number, still… hope is a hard beast to dampen. I glance at the screen. Hope gets put out pretty damn quick.

'Bad news?' Nelly asks, leaning towards me.

'The worst. Betsy wants to see me on Thursday.'

'I don't know.' Nelly slides his chair back. I think I've outstayed my welcome. He's going to want to get back to that model with the dress she can barely breathe in before the poor woman asphyxiates. 'It might not all be bad,' he says. 'You need to talk to the board. You're not a one-man band anymore. And you do have to get back into that building.'

Don't I know it. But none of that matters. I don't care about the business. I know that Fitz will pull it through. She might wear a wacky airhead exterior, but the woman has a heart of gold and a good business head on her shoulders. Betsy probably hasn't realised it yet, but Fitz never stays in the background for long. Still, that doesn't solve my problem.

'I've got to find her, Nelly,' I groan. 'Do you have an address for her?'

'Oh, Marco.' He takes my hands in his. 'No. No, I have nothing. But…' Suddenly, his eyes fire up, bright as sparklers. 'I do have an idea where she might be.'

'Yeah?' I'm on my feet.

'There's this odd little café, an all-night joint by the looks of it. Smithfield Market. She seemed to be in there with a guy.' He pauses. 'Friend *guy*,' he adds for clarification.

'Blond hair? Five ten? On the scrawny side?'

Nelly nods. 'Got him. It seemed like he was a regular. I'm pretty sure someone will know where she is if you head there.'

It's worth a try.

CLARA

Evelyn's looking washed-out. We've been practising since seven thirty, ever since she put Thea down.

'Just put the air behind it. You need a little more support on the notes. It's breathy, yes, but you don't want to flip it too far that way. It's casual. Lift the soft palate less. More relaxed, but clear and strong.'

'It's no good.' I flop down onto her comfy sofa. 'I just can't get it. Can we try an easier song? Avoid the high notes?'

Evelyn fans a heap of assorted sheet music out in front of us, spreading it across the floor. The task seems hopeless. There's almost too much. Where do we even start?

'It needs to be something easy,' Evelyn says as she scans the vocal scores. 'Something you feel comfortable with, but something that shows off your voice.'

Practically all the stuff we do for the choir is religious. Hymns and things. I'm not sure that's going to cut it for this audition.

'The problem is...' Evelyn says, running her eyes anxiously over the notes. 'The arrangement, the way you sang the original song, it was different. It had that element of originality. A bit of you. That's what they want. Only now, they've heard your demo track. They're going to need something else.'

'"Amazing Grace"?'

Evelyn shakes her head. 'Even I know that's not going to cut the mustard. It's got to be something modern. They're a music production company.'

'We don't have time,' I sob. It would be fine if I were confident, but I don't like singing in public. It's never going to work.

'I think you go in with a Kiri Matalixa.'

'No way.' Kiri has been blocking the charts for the past twelve months. She has the golden larynx and an attitude to match. 'She's a belter. I can't do that.'

Evelyn sinks to her knees. 'Clara, you're going to have to try. It's not just about you getting a record deal. If you can't prove to that Betsy fire-breathing dragon woman that you were staying up all night using the studio's equipment, Marco's going to be in big trouble.'

She's right. 'Okay, let's try the Kiri.'

MARCO

I've managed to down two breakfast baps and five mugs of tea. It's nine o'clock at night. I'm sitting in Jack's, twiddling my thumbs, waiting for the mystery guy to turn up. If this doesn't work, I guess I'll have to try to sneak into the Towers, although

I'm going in on Thursday. Tomorrow's Wednesday. Instead of taking my lift up to the seventeenth floor, I could stop by the front desk. I'm pretty sure the door guy knows Clara. He could get a message to her. Maybe I should write her a note. I tap my pockets. I have no paper. Why the hell is life so complicated?

'You sure do like those baps,' Jack says, lifting the plate from my table.

If I sit here much longer, I'll be on for a coronary.

'Best in town,' I say, wiping the ketchup from my fingers. 'You don't have a bit of paper, do you? I need to write a letter.'

He laughs. 'That's quaint. A love letter?'

'Not really.' I shift in my seat uncomfortably.

'Doesn't she have a phone?'

'I didn't say it was a she.' I'm beginning to wish I hadn't said anything to Jack, anything bar a compliment about his bacon.

'I can give you a napkin. Very romantic, napkins. Drinks coasters are better if it's a swanky bar, a bar with kudos. But you can't fit much on a coaster. You can get a hell of a lot on a napkin if you don't press too hard. Have you got a lot to write?'

I sigh. 'Not sure. Think so.'

'Then you're definitely best with a napkin.' He goes to the grill station and pulls out three, smoothing them down with his hand before passing them to me.

'And…' He pulls a pen from behind his ear. 'You'll be needing this.'

'Thanks,' I say, grasping the pen firmly and lining up the napkin as he walks away.

I'm not good at this. The only real relationship I had, or thought I had, was with Fitz, and that was born out of growing up together. We were literally thrown together, and then parental pressure and expectations kept us there. There was never really any choice. What I'm feeling now is different. Less than a week ago, I met the most amazing woman in the history of the universe: beautiful, kind, funny, intelligent. The kind of woman you want to be with for the rest of your life, and it all went so well. So brilliantly. That night at the gala, it couldn't have gone better. If I hadn't had to run off to protect her from Fitz's parents, it would have all worked out okay. A letter is the only way I can get across exactly what I'm feeling. I start to write, making sure not to press too hard.

Hi Clara,

I know this is kind of strange. We've only just met, but since that day in my office, my whole world has been tipped upside down. I'm sorry we had to part so suddenly at the gala. That would not have been my choice. I would never have given you up. I just wanted to protect you. Works gone...

I pause. Can I write batshit?

'You okay, Shakespeare?' Jack asks as he cleans down the grill.

'Yeah, just wondering, can I put work has gone batshit? I mean, is that okay?'

Jack stops with the grill scraping, sucks in his cheeks as he mulls it over. 'I'm not sure you want to bring work up in a love letter.'

'Well, it's more of an apology. A declaration of intent.'

'Intent.' Jack nods. 'I think batshit's fine.'

I write *batshit* and *call me* and add my number.

'Done?' Jack asks.

'Done.' I fold it into my pocket and pull my cigarettes out.

'Oh no. Not in here, mate.'

'Course.' I stand, pushing back my chair. 'Is it okay if I leave my stuff at the table?' I indicate back to my chair, my coat, my bag.

'Knock yourself out,' Jack says.

Wearily I head out onto the street. Most of the shops are closed, and there's a late summer nip in the air. Directly opposite, the last greengrocer is taking in his veg, pulling down the awning, getting ready to wind down the blinds. I take a cigarette from its packet. I don't really smoke. Not anymore. Not much. As I get my lighter out I wonder if Clara smokes. I could give up. I can give up tomorrow. I'll deliver the letter on Wednesday. Probably, I'll transfer it and put it on some better paper. Maybe get some nice stuff. Nelly has nice stuff. I could always... Then out of the corner of my eye, I see him. The scrawny blond-haired man. The valet parking guy. The guy who knows her. He's heading towards Jack's. Just before he's about to step onto the road, he turns his head to shoot a line of banter to the guy packing his veg away. It's just a line. I don't catch it, but what I do see is the van. The van reversing into the street, reversing into the path of the valet guy.

'Stop!' I shout. But he doesn't, and the van doesn't. In a split second, without thinking, I lunge into the road. The valet guy looks at me. His eyes widening as my outstretched hands hit him hard in the chest and he falls back into the stall. Veg is flying. I'm flying. Nothing is right. And then everything is dark. Very dark.

CHAPTER 18

CLARA

I'm standing outside Delagado Towers. It's Thursday. I've stood here many times before. So many times, I've crossed the road, said hi to Stan, and got on with my day. Only this particular Thursday, I'm terrified.

'Are you sure I look all right?' I say, winding the ends of my hair around my finger, curing them for about the hundredth time into place.

Evelyn places both hands supportively on my shoulders as though willing strength into me. 'You look great, Clara. Seriously great.'

I nod but I don't feel great. 'I'm wearing the blue wrap dress I wore the first day I went up to the seventeenth floor. Maybe I should have bought something new, but I just felt I needed to keep it simple. I had this overwhelming idea to keep things comfortable, as familiar as possible. This was going to be difficult enough as it was. If I was to be perfectly honest, I'm not sure I even want to sing professionally anymore. I love singing with the choir and singing with friends. I had even loved my taster of working in the music industry. Well, loved it until it all went belly up. I guess my focus has shifted; this is all about clearing Marco's name.

'Clara,' Evelyn says firmly, pulling me back to the here and now. 'I'm not coming up, but Fitz will be there and you said you know Terry and Jeff. You know everyone. Just don't let Betsy put you off.'

I feel sick. I can barely speak, let alone sing. 'I won't let Betsy get to me,' I say, crossing my fingers behind my back.

Evelyn draws me into a hug before turning me around as though I'm a robot and pointing me towards the door. I see Stan's smiling face.

'You'll be fine,' Evelyn whispers into my ear, and off I set, walking across the landscaped entrance to the doors.

'Hey,' Stan calls out, a look of absolute delight on his face. 'Jeez, we missed you. Are you back for good?'

'Oh, Stan.' I feel my calmness crumbling. 'I've got to go and sing.'

'About time, too,' Stan says, swinging open the door.

'But I'm terrified,' I say. I can feel my shoulders rising. The tension is unbearable.

'You've got to push yourself,' he says as he walks me through the vast marble foyer. 'Fitz has told me exactly what's happening. That Betsy Miller, she's a problem. If she gets control of the company, she's going to asset strip. All the Delagado businesses, everything, will be sold off.'

'No pressure then.'

He laughs. 'You're only doing what comes natural, songbird.' He presses the golden button and the lift doors slide open. 'Be here when you get down to earth.' Then he does the sweetest thing. Stan takes my hand, squeezes it gently, and says, 'Don't worry how it goes. We got you.'

I stagger into the lift. For a long moment, the doors remain open, Stan on the outside looking in, grinning from ear to ear, me on the inside wishing I could make a run for it. As the lift whirs, the doors shut, and I can feel the mechanism outside pulling me up to the seventeenth floor. I feel sure that my knees are actually sinking. That I'm somehow going in the opposite direction. When they finally come to a halt, and when those knees finally come to a halt, the lift doors start to open and I allow myself a deep breath. I have to do this. It's not just for Marco now; it's for Stan, for Fitz, for Terry and Jeff, for everyone in the building.

'Great,' Betsy says. She's standing outside the lift door and glances at her watch. 'Well, at least you're on time.'

'Oh, stop fussing, Betsy,' I hear Fitz drawl. 'I took the stairs. Haven't you ever heard of cardiovascular exercise? We said we would be here. We are.'

Betsy glances at her watch again. 'All apart from Marco, it would seem.'

'We'll wait,' Fitz says casually, flopping her Birkenstock bag down on the reception desk.

'We can't,' Betsy says, folding her arms. She's as inflexible as a buffalo grill.

'Oh come on, Betsy,' Fitz says, walking off toward the studio, flicking her hair into place. 'Terry and Jeff won't mind if Marco's a bit late. He'll get here…' Suddenly, she stops. She's looking into the studio. There's a guy in there, one I don't recognise, with the coolest looks and the fanciest diamond guitar. Fitz points one long finger towards the window. 'Is that who I think it is?'

Betsy nods smugly. 'Jackson Black.'

Fitz's eyes practically ping-pong out of her head, as her mouth drops open. 'Here, but what's he…?' Suddenly her elation cools. 'And where are Terry and Jeff?'

Betsy narrows her eyes. 'You just missed them.'

Fitz shoots back to the reception desk and digs out her phone. It's full to the brim with messages. 'I don't…' She flicks through them, a look of total confusion on her face.

My knees are still not functioning properly. I can't cope with

Jackson Black; the man is mega. I slump down on the red leather sofa.

'No time to sit,' Betsy says, waggling a hand towards me, indicating I should stand.

'Betsy,' Fitz says, her voice bubbling with suppressed anger. 'What have you done?'

'We're going to have a proper recording session.'

'But you can't get rid of Jeff and Terry,' Fitz says, her voice still sounding shell-shocked.

'Oh, Fitz.' Betsy laughs. It's not a nice laugh. It's over-syrupy and yet as hard as ice. 'I haven't let them go.' There's a slight pause, one I bet Betsy is itching to interject a 'not yet' into. 'I've just given them the afternoon off.'

'But…' Fitz looks like she's going to scream.

But sadly, the more emotional Fitz looks, the calmer Betsy seems to become.

'Clara suffers from nerves,' Fitz says, waving one long arm out towards me.

I clear my throat, feeling like a piece of extra baggage. 'I was hoping it would be Terry and Jeff in the studio. It would be less daunting.'

Betsy's eyes narrow. 'So, if you were playing at the O2 or Hyde Park, or the Albert Hall, you'd want them there for that?'

I feel my shoulders drawing tighter and tighter. All the work I'd been doing on my breathing, on keeping calm, it's all wasted.

'Is there a problem?' I turn to see Jackson Black standing in the studio doorway.

'No,' I say, taking in a deep breath.

'Good.' He nods slowly and raps his fingers against the doorframe. 'Because time is money.'

'Ain't that right,' Betsy says.

I feel Fitz's hand on my arm. 'Are you okay, Clara? We could do it another time?'

Betsy throws her hands up to her head. It's total melodrama, but scary with it. 'Another time? I thought we were here to clear Margo Delagado's name!'

Suddenly I realise that, actually, a lot of the Delagado branding has gone from the studio. The logo on the desk has been picked off. The corporate stationery seems to have disappeared. It hasn't taken long for Betsy to attempt a full take over.

'It's not a problem,' I say, projecting a coolness I am absolutely not feeling. Shall we start?' I walk into the recording studio.

Jackson Black nods. 'No time like the present.'

I shuffle in my shoes, stand in front of the mic, fill my lungs, and my world cracks in half.

❧

I run straight from the studio to the washroom. I think I mumbled something before I sprinted, or maybe I mumbled it as my shoes were streaking across the carpet. But if I did, I can't remember what it might have been. As I sit on the closed lid of the toilet, tears streaming down my face, my breathing is so erratic I can barely hold enough air in my lungs to support the most basic functioning of a human body, let alone allow it to sing. I am a fool, a first-class fool.

'Hey.' There's a gentle rap on the door. 'It's Fitz. You okay in there?'

'I'm so sorry. I let you down,' I gasp. 'I let everyone down. But I promise that voice, the missing…' I can barely say the words. I detest that whole label so much. 'That missing songbird. It is me. Just like I said.' Sheepishly, I open the door. Fitz is standing there, a pained smile on her face.

'You were pretty shit just now.'

I sob. 'Sorry, I…'

'Hey.' She shrugs. 'Actually, you were so shit that I totally believe you. I believe you about creeping into the studio. I absolutely one hundred per cent believe you about the singing solo bit.' She sighs. 'I wish we had those damn CCTV recordings. Betsy's so smug, I seriously want to bite her nose off.'

I can't help it, I laugh. 'Her nose?'

'Yeah. I know it's odd, but it would totally blindside the woman, so it would be so worth it.' Fitz runs her eyes appraisingly over my face and scowls. 'You look like you've had a fight with a hedge and the hedge came off best.' She leans forward and picks a thick false eyelash from my cheek and holds it between her index finger and thumb as if it's some weird new creature. 'I think these are supposed to go on your eyelids?'

Leaning back into the stall, I grab the end of a roll of toilet paper and pull myself off a wodge, dabbing the paper under my eyes as I flush away the offending eyelash creature. 'What will happen to Marco? To the business. Did you see she's taken down all the logos?' I say, finally feeling brave enough to step out of the stall.

Fitz moves back, leaning against the sinks. 'That woman has seriously got some nerve. But don't worry too much, I'll get some damage limitation in place.'

'After you bite off her nose?'

She smirks. 'Don't tell anyone I told you that. Are you going to be okay to get home?'

'Yeah, I'll call my brother.' But the thought of seeing Minty when I'm in this state suddenly worries me. He'll just get totally overprotective. I don't think I can cope with all the male posturing. 'Or maybe,' I say, 'maybe I'll just get a taxi.'

'Good idea,' Fitz says kindly. Rubbing my shoulder in a supportive squeeze before placing both her thumbs beneath my eyes and giving them a quick sweep clean-up. 'There, that's better, and…' She digs in her bag, magicking out a tube of concealer. 'A little help for under those eyes.' She waggles the tube in the air. 'It's got this amazing hush-hush anti-puff ingredient.' Fitz examines my eyes. 'But you're going to put the stuff absolutely through its paces.' She tilts her head thoughtfully to one side. 'If you do social media, this would be a good opportunity to do a before and after shot.'

No way am I going to let any living creature get a peek at my 'before'. I take the tube, twist the silver lid, and pull out the gloop-coated wand. I'm not sure the secret ingredient is going to be able to cope with this much mess, but anything's worth a try. 'What did Jackson Black say?' I ask, delicately painting the creased, red folds under both eyes.

Fitz raps her nails against the porcelain of the sink. 'You don't want to know.'

I glance at her.

'Okay, a lot about professionalism. A whole heap about talent not being what it used to be and something mildly complimentary about your blue dress.' She shrugs.

'Two out of three's not bad.'

She grins. 'I like your style.'

I hand her back the concealer, feeling a lot more human.

'I'll come out with you,' she says, tucking the make-up into her bag. 'I can distract the dragon while you go down in the lift.'

I lean forward and give her a big hug. 'Thanks, Fitz.'

'Hey.' she laughs. 'That was nothing. It's what friends are for.'

And I can't help but smile. This woman is an absolute sweetheart.

As I descend in the golden lift, I realise I don't ever want to be in a studio again. I wish I could have cleared Marco's name. Cleared it totally, but maybe that CCTV footage will turn up. If it does, it will be obvious to everyone that it was me who went into the studio. That he wasn't there and I went in of my own free will. I kind of wish Marco would turn up, too. I realise with an odd sinking sensation in my chest that despite the humiliation, the sheer terror I felt when standing there taking the mic and warbling with an uncontrolled fear in a high-tech sound studio in front of music legend Jackson Black, the thing I found most disappointing was that Marco wasn't there. I miss him. Miss the excitement I feel when he walks into a room, as if every moment of life has more energy. Shines brighter. When the lift doors slide back, I'm half expecting to see Stan with that large, sloppy grin over his face. I'm half dreading it too. I'm going to have to tell him I just made a total and utter fool of myself. I wonder if we still have that old goblin mask under the desk. I would put the damn thing on so I could escape unnoticed out of the building, but the foyer seems eerily quiet. There's no one. It's as if some kind of movie disaster has happened. One that removes everybody from the planet apart from one person. Me. I can actually hear the low hum of electricity pulsing through the marble hallway.

'Stan?' I call out, hesitantly moving out of the lift and into the foyer. The cool air-conditioned air makes my skin prickle. I glance towards the desk, my old desk, wondering if he's hiding there, waiting to jump out and growl at me. But no... there's no one.

I look at the bank of phones. They're completely silent. Not one light flashing, demanding to be re-routed. Did I miss the memo that said 'Evaporation Day on Thursday'? I walk through the hall; my shoes, the comfortable but pretty ones with the red straps and the hint of toe cleave, echo as I step slowly across the space.

A large, uncontrolled part of me wants to run. Kick off my shoes and sprint hell for leather towards the door and out of this place. Towards the garden outside and its bubbling brook, talk grasses, flowers and shade, dappling trees – with its carefully curated normality. But I just walk. Confused.

I push the door open and step out, following the path slowly as it curves me out from the marble magnificence of the foyer into the landscaped steel and glass exterior of the Towers. Then it hits me. The garden. That's where everyone is. Stan and Evelyn are smiling, grinning ear to ear, beckoning me towards them. But it's not just Stan and Evelyn. No, it's so much more. It's my entire choir.

'Hey, songbird,' Stan calls, extending his arm for me to take.

'We thought you might get nervous,' Evelyn explains.

'We all wanted to be here for you.' One of the other choir members squeezes my arm.

I feel overwhelmed. These people are so sweet. They actually care.

'Come on,' Evelyn says gently. 'You know what the best thing to do is when you've had a shock?'

'No,' I say, wiping away a tear.

'Get back on that horse.' Evelyn laughs, turning back towards the choir. 'Ladies, are we ready?'

'Yes!' they all cheer.

'Terry, Jeff?' Evelyn glances over towards a raised dais. It's all set up for recording. Jeff rushes over and clips a small mic to the fold of my wrap dress. You would barely know the thing is there.

'You got this,' he says, shooting me a wink.

'No pressure,' Evelyn says, taking up position in front of the smiling choir, 'but if you feel like going for the solo, Clara, just nod, and we'll all back out.'

There's a supportive murmur from the crowd.

Jeff hits the intro, and I open my mouth and sing.

I stop worrying about who will hear, why I'm doing this, and what's at stake. I just sing. My voice soars with my heart. As the last notes flow freely from my mouth, and the ripple of applause bounces off the buildings, I turn to see Fitz standing next to Betsy. Fitz gives me the thumbs up. Even Jackson Black gives me the thumbs up. There's no doubt that I'm the missing songbird.

As the choir disperse, each person gives me a hug before they rush off for their busy lives of school pick-ups, ageing parents, food to be made or consumed. I catch Fitz loitering with Terry and make my way over. They're laughing together. She's batting her long lashes at him, and he's beaming. Are they an item? I hadn't realised. So she's genuinely not interested in Marco. I sidle up to her. She pulls back self-consciously, indulging in an over-generous exuberance, which is maybe intended to cover up something she didn't want me to see.

'You were fantastic. Amazing.'

'Thank you,' I say, trying to stop the colour rising from my cheeks. It's okay to accept compliments. I have to learn to do that better. But that's not my only concern. 'So I'm guessing Marco's not going to have to face any charges of impropriety,' I say.

Fitz shakes her head, delighted, her streaked black hair falling over her face. 'Absolutely not. In fact, after you left, they found the missing files.'

'Oh?'

Fitz raises one eyebrow. 'Down the back of Betsy's desk. She must have pushed it there by accident when she thought the place had been burgled.'

'Thought?' I say, perplexed. I thought it most definitely had been burgled.

'Yup. *Thought*. We found the CCTV footage in Marco's bin. To be honest…' She clutches both hands in front of her, her head slipping to one side in a childish, charming manner. 'You didn't need to sing. We saw you go in. But…' She grabs my shoulder. 'We loved your singing. It was fun because it really rubbed the whole thing in so nicely for Betsy.' Fitz's eyes flash with a cheeky exuberance.

'So Marco's off the hook.' My body relaxes.

'Hmm…' Fitz points the toe of her expensive trainer into the soft boards of the dais. 'Not completely. He took the guitars.'

I can't believe what I'm hearing. 'Honestly?'

She nods. 'Oh yeah. It's plain as day. I mean, he's wearing a hoody but,' she throws her hands up in a comic show of exasperation before lowering her voice, 'it's the one he always wears, so…'

I take a deep breath and exhale slowly, my heart racing in my chest. So all of this was for nothing. Betsy still has dirt on Marco. A frown crosses my forehead as it hits me. 'Fitz, where is Marco?'

CHAPTER 19

CLARA

'You would not believe the past couple of days I've had,' Minty says.

I don't have time for this. We're in the kitchen. It's a mess. 'Me too, Minty, but it doesn't mean that I don't keep things organised at home.'

He pulls out one of the pine kitchen chairs from under the table and sinks onto it. 'That's because you're amazing.'

'No.' Sometimes he makes me so mad. 'It's because I'm organised. I don't let one little thing like an oil change upset my universe.'

He stops rubbing his temples and gives me an odd look, as if realising for the first time that life does not actually revolve around him.

'I could get a takeaway for us tonight?' This is Minty's answer to everything.

'I don't want a takeaway.' I don't want to eat. I want to get things sorted in the house and then hit the sack. I'd love to sleep, but I've started to worry. No one has seen any trace of Marco. Not for forty-eight hours. Then there's the missing guitars, Betsy still on the warpath, and nothing is right.

'I've got this new mate,' Minty says, picking the oil out of his cuticles, 'that I think would be perfect for you.'

'Minty, no! Not after the last one. No way. And don't do that with your hands. We eat at that table.'

He sighs, leaning back in his chair, running both of his palms down the full length of his face. 'Ugh.'

'I want to get back to the office. Stan said he'll try to help me trace Marco. He knows a driver that Marco uses. I know it's stupid; he'd contact me if he wanted to, but… I need to see him again, just once. Have you got any washing to do?' I ask Minty.

He groans. 'You don't have to.'

'I'm putting on a wash. Anything blue. Nothing oily.'

Minty pulls himself from the table and ambles up the stairs. 'I don't feel like I've seen much of you recently,' he says, his voice growing thinner as he reaches the landing.

My brother's right. We've sort of become like valet cars passing in the night. I want to tell him what's happening at work, but I'm not even sure I can explain it. Certainly not to a simple soul like my brother.

'Here,' he says, ambling back into the kitchen and dumping a pair of filthy jeans and a sweatshirt on the kitchen table.

'Not where we eat, Minty,' I say, pushing the bundle onto the chair he left out when he took his leave from the table.

'Sorry,' he says, his voice sounding a little hurt.

I sigh. 'No, I'm sorry.' I run a hand through my hair. Knotting it back into the tortoise shell clip I've been wearing since I got in. I'd spent ages curling it before I went out. I spent hours trying to get my image right. Then I opened my mouth in the studio and… I give my head a quick shake. I don't want to think about that. Besides, once I was in the choir, I sang like an angel – Jackson Black's words, not my own. 'Have you checked the pockets?' I say, grabbing hold of the jeans.

'Aw.' Minty hits his head with the palm of his hand. 'Next time.'

'Next time,' I repeat, knowing the exact same scenario will happen again the next time. My brother is nothing, if not predictable. I stick my hand in his jeans and draw out a tissue. 'See.' I waggle the thing in front of his eyes. 'If this goes in the wash, it breaks up. I have to clean the drum and…' Suddenly, I realise there are dark stains all over the tissue. It's not a tissue, it's a napkin. The dark stains are… 'Minty,' I say, trying to keep the horror out of my voice. 'Is this blood?'

He glances at the napkin. 'Oh yeah. I think it might be, sorry.'

'What… your blood?'

'No.' He pulls the napkin from my fingers. 'The guy that got knocked down.'

'What?'

'Yeah.' He gives me a wary, disbelieving smile. 'You would not believe what kind of a…'

'Jack's?' I say, reading the logo on the napkin and snatching it back.

'Yeah.' Minty nods. 'I was just crossing the road to…'

But whatever Minty was saying fades into the background as I open the napkin and see there's a letter written on it. A letter to me, from a man who's sorry. Who says that the night at the gala didn't end in the way he wanted it to. That he was protecting me. That work has gone crazy, and I'm the only good thing left in his life.

'Minty!' I say, clutching the napkin to my chest. 'I've got to meet this guy.'

My brother's eyes brighten with absolute joy. 'Sis, that's exactly what I'm trying to tell you. You seriously have to. This guy saved my life. You will love him.'

MARCO

'I've messed up.' This goes without saying, since I'm lying in a hospital bed with an IV sticking out of my arm, a broken leg, and one arm in a cast.

'Well…' Fitz shifts awkwardly on the hard plastic seat. She's munching her way through the grapes that she bought me, which is fine. I don't want grapes. I want someone to give me a rollicking. Tell me what an idiot I've been.

Fitz swallows hard. 'Most of the Betsy balls-up has been kind of,' she waves one arm in a so-so gesture, 'sorted. Not sure your songbird will ever sing solo again, though.'

At the mention of Clara, my whole body has a surge of adrenaline. 'I can't believe you put her through that.'

Fitz shrugs, kicks off her shoes and places her dainty painted toes on my immaculate hospital sheets. 'I didn't know she had some kind of phobia.'

Nor did I. Anyone who had heard that voice on the tape would have thought they were hearing a consummate professional, someone who could slide into any of the main music venues worldwide.

'Besides, the choir was sweet.' Fitz waggles one toe, kneels towards it and flicks off a fleck of paint. 'Might even join myself.' Suddenly she pulls her legs back, slips her feet back into her shoes, and leans forward. A note of seriousness weighs down her features. 'There's still the problem with the missing guitars.'

'Those were mine,' I say, feeling irritated. 'My dad gave them to me.'

She chews her bottom lip. 'You have a record of that?'

'Course not. He's my dad. Parents just give kids things.'

'Hmm.' She places her head on one side. 'Yeah, but there are things like balloons and birthday cakes and roller skates, and then there are things like yachts, penthouses, and Heritage guitars.'

I pull one hand through the patches of my hair that are still available without the decoration of white bandages. I can see maybe this is a bit of a problem.

'And then you did kind of let everyone think they were stolen.'

'That was because Betsy was going on and on about it.'

Fitz pouts. 'So, you thought you'd jump on the bandwagon?'

I sigh. 'Fitz, I just want to get out. I don't want to produce music anymore. I don't want to find the next big voice. I want a simple life. Play my own guitar. Do a few gigs every week. Read the paper. Get a dog. Get a life.'

She bites her lip, clearly trying hard not to smile. 'Get a Clara.'

'No, I–'

'Oh, come on.' She laughs. 'It is so obvious. Besides, I like her.'

'Great,' I say, glad of any approval I can get. 'Only I'm not sure she feels the same way about me. Not now anyway.' I sigh, edging my body into the mattress a little deeper, wondering why I can't get comfortable. Oh course, that would be because my body got hit by a truck. 'I messed things up at the gala.'

Fitz frowns. 'You messed more things up?'

I shoot her an irritated look.

Suddenly, her face looks deadly serious as she takes her hand between mine and stares into my eyes. 'You've got to stop the drinking.'

'But I-I…' I stutter, my hand shooting up in protest.

'Ughh uh.' She shakes her head. 'Not good enough. Not anymore. No excuses. You need to get yourself straight.'

I can feel myself bristling. 'It's not as if I can knock anything back in here.'

'Marco, drink is messing with your life. This girl is great, wonderful. I genuinely do like her. She doesn't deserve a weekend drunk.'

She's right. Okay, so maybe I'm not an alcoholic, or at least not a regular drinker, but the binge drinking is messing up my life. If Clara was in it, I'd want everything to be perfect. I feel a wave of disappointment.

'Yeah, you're talking like we're a thing. We're not. I don't even know how she really feels about me.'

'Oh come on, Marco.' Fitz gets to her feet, leans forward and plants a kiss on my forehead. 'Just tell her how you feel. That's all you have to do. It's a great start, and don't worry about the,' she waves one arm, attaching the back of her sling-backs into place with the other, 'work thing. I don't want you back.' She smiles. 'I think I can pull it off. Find the voice. Manage the office. Deal with Betsy and the guitars. Bring them back when you're ready. I'll draw you up a chit, saying you've loaned them to us. Get everything above board.'

'Wow,' I say, laughing. 'You really have got the whole thing figured out.'

She squeezes my arm. 'So have you. In your own way. You just need to tell her.'

Easier said than done. I watch Fitz swagger away, smiling at the other sick people on the ward. They all smile back, putty in her hands. I kind of wish I'd realised what a force that woman was before, but I have to admire her for keeping it quiet. Some people are all shop windows, whereas others run deep. Fitz runs deeper than the Marianna Trench, which is thirty-five thousand feet deep and counting – so pretty deep!

CHAPTER 20

MARCO

'I have had the most bonkers day.'

The guy I saved from the truck, well, okay, not truck, transit van, is sitting in the exact same place as Fitz had been sitting only hours before. He's an odd chap but always glass half full. In fact, more like glass flowing over. I get the feeling it would be impossible to burst his balloon. I have no intention of asking why he's had such a bonkers day. I've only known him for three days. Sadly, these three days have been on the trot. Once in the ambulance as we sped towards the hospital. The second time was the following morning when he came in smelling of diesel oil and carrying flowers, which was kind of sweet especially as no one's ever bought me flowers before. And then today. So, three times total, and every single time he's told me that he's had the most bonkers day. The man should be in my shoes. His name's Minty. Which in itself is a bit odd. Because he's not Minty, anything but. Each time he comes in, I can see the nurses worrying about where he'll sit and what he'll touch.

'I did buy you a little something,' Minty says, putting a wrapped bacon sandwich onto my sheets. 'Jack sends his love. And Lennie and the greengrocers.' He pulls a stack of fruit from his other pocket. 'You're a hero, to be honest Everyone saw you do the dive. Man, I wish I had it on camera. You practically flew.'

I certainly flew after the van hit me.

Minty looks around the ward, smiling at all the other people that are laid up. Most of them ignore him. 'I mean, mate.' He grabs my hand, looking earnestly into my eyes. 'You're the best.'

'Thanks,' I say. 'Anyone would have done it.'

He laughs. 'No, no. You are a star, and…' He clears his throat. 'How do you feel about dating?'

Oh no. I feel my heart sink. This cannot be happening. I knew this guy was getting too close. 'Actually Minty, I–'

'Only, my sister…'

I feel relief flood over me.

'Yeah, I honestly think,' he continues eagerly. 'You and my sister–'

'Actually, Minty…' I know I've got to stop this. I don't want affairs. I don't want one-night stands. I don't want to be sandwiched into everyone else's idea of what or who I should date. 'I've got my eye on someone really special. Sorry, mate.' I glance around the ward and then suddenly my heart sings. It literally rises up and blocks my throat, pushing aside any ideas of what I was about to say, or any urgency to say it, because it's her. Clara.

'Marco,' she says, standing there, as if singled out from the entire world. Singled out for me.

'I'm so sorry,' I say. 'I didn't mean to run off.'

She waves something in her right hand. A napkin? 'I got your note. It was kind of…' She opens it out. 'Written in blood, so I knew you meant it.'

I reach forward, pain shooting down my right side, but I don't care, I just have to hold her, touch her. She grabs my hand. 'Oh, and I see you've met my brother.' She nods towards Minty.

'Seriously?' I do a double-take.

'Yeah.' She smiles. 'He washes up okay.'

Minty laughs. 'You see, sis, I told you. I told you I could find you the right man.'

I kind of wish I hadn't had to take the brute force of a speeding van in order for that to happen, but then again…

She sinks into my arms. 'I hear you've left your job?'

'Fitz is taking over. She's got Amy back in and helping out. Can't believe I treated Amy so badly. But she forgave me.'

'She's a sweetheart like that. Fitz and Amy, the dream team. They'll be fantastic.'

'Don't I know it. Fitz bought all my shares. So she's the big boss now. Betsy's going to have to keep her hands off, and Fitz is happy. She loves work and is pretty partial to Terry.'

Clara laughs. 'Happy endings all around.'

I shrug. 'Exactly. It was time for me to step back, but I hear you've stopped pursuing a career in music?'

'Hmmm. I've decided I want something more down to earth. High-rise living, it isn't all it's cracked up to be. But I still want to sing in the shower.'

I draw her towards me and kiss her soft lips. 'Now that, I want to see.'

CHAPTER 21

CLARA

'Where are you off to then?' the cabbie says as he loads my two suitcases into his black cab. 'A jaunt away for a bit of sun?'

'Not quite,' I say as, standing there on the pavement, I give my brother a long hug.

'You'll be fine, C,' Minty says, holding me so tight I feel the air flatten out of my lungs. 'Any problems, your room will always be here.'

We both glance at the house we grew up in. There are so many memories contained within those four walls.

I've made sure the freezer is fully stocked. I've dredged the last corners of the washing basket, and the airing cupboard has had every towel and sheet and tea towel folded or pressed. I hope Minty is going to be all right without me. He says he will, and you never know, without me in the house, maybe he'll even get brave enough to bring a few girls back. Never mind my love life, in looking after me, I kind of feel he may have forgotten to get his own.

I choke back the tears. 'You know I love you, Minty,' I mumble between sobs.

He holds me at arm's length so he can see into my eyes. 'And there's me thinking, all those years, that you were here for the cheap rent.'

I laugh.

As the taxi pulls away, I wave back at Minty till my arm aches.

'Hate those goodbyes,' the cabbie says sagely.

'Yup.' I pull an already damp tissue over my tear-streaked cheeks.

The driver glances at my mess of a face in the rectangle of his mirror. 'But it's time to move on, eh?'

'You got it.' I smile sadly, glancing out of the window as the area I love flits past. When Marco said to me, 'Why don't we take it slowly?' I didn't quite get it at first, but now I can't wait to start.

As my car pulls up at the marina, I catch sight of the man I love standing on one of the long pontoons flanking the water, and still, after all this time, my heart beats ten to the dozen when I see him. I can't ever imagine losing that excitement, although I have to admit, our romance was certainly not all plain sailing. Learning curve might be a better description. Marco healed up fine after the accident. All the broken bones are mended, and some of the things that neither of us knew even needed to be fixed, like our terrible communication skills, ironed themselves out with a little practice. Getting rid of the stress of work, the pretence of being someone that he's not, allowed a whole different kind of Marco to emerge. He plays the music he likes on an acoustic guitar. Just a cheap one he picked up on Gumtree. There's a lot of enjoyment to be found when life doesn't have to be designer perfect, when you can just be true to yourself. I know he feels better now waking up clear-headed, after choosing herbal tea over whisky in the evening. The twelve-step meetings in the church basement had been harder than any board meeting for Marco, but they'd given him something the music industry never could: an ability to be honest with himself. Moving forward, I know he will have to make a daily choice to stay sober, but I'm going to be with him, not trying to fix him, but being there while he fixes himself.

I jump out of the taxi and wave excitedly to him.

Instantly, he's striding towards me, a massive smile on that cheeky chiselled face of his.

I'm barely able to keep my feet from dancing on the hard stone quay of the dock as we glance out over the marina. There are so many boats. 'So, which one's ours?' I ask.

'Only the best for my beautiful songbird,' he says, taking my hand in his and kissing the bridge of my knuckles as if he never wants to let me go.

Then I see it. I see it because the boat is covered in 'Just Married' bunting and lights – a double Dutch barge, Tiffany blue, with a canopy at the back.

'Married?' I say, my eyes narrowing.

'Sure, why not? Nelly left you a dress in one of the cabins.'

I clap like an excited child.

'And I knew you wouldn't go through the whole thing without your brother and the entire entourage, so they're set to meet us at St Anne's in around,' he glances at his watch, 'an hour or so.' He looks deeply into my eyes. 'That is, if you say yes.'

I smile so wide my jaw aches. 'Does that boat have running water and a power point for my hair tongs?'

'Is this the 21st century?'

'Yes. Yes. Yes, to all of it. I love it,' I squeal as he picks me up and twirls me around. 'I love you, the boat, the open water. This is absolutely the perfect harmony.'

And he kisses me because he can hear it too, we both can: the best tune on the entire planet. The absolute winner – the notes between us, the one thing that keeps the whole world turning, notes made up of friendship, family and love.

ALSO BY SHIRLEY DAY

Person of Interest

The Insect House

Reap What You Sow

www.ingramcontent.com/pod-product-compliance
Lightning Source LLC
Chambersburg PA
CBHW021544300126
38837CB00045B/1066

* 9 7 8 1 9 1 7 7 0 5 6 3 9 *

A NOTE FROM THE PUBLISHER

Thank you for reading this book. If you enjoyed it please do consider leaving a review on Amazon to help others find it too.

We hate typos. All of our books have been rigorously edited and proofread, but sometimes mistakes do slip through. If you have spotted a typo, please do let us know and we can get it amended within hours.

info@bloodhoundbooks.com